THE TAIL OF
AUGUSTUS MOON

The Tail Of Augustus Moon

by

Melanie Whitehouse

Dales Large Print Books
Long Preston, North Yorkshire,
BD23 4ND, England.

British Library Cataloguing in Publication Data

Whitehouse, Melanie
   The tail of Augustus Moon.

      A catalogue record of this book is
      available from the British Library

   ISBN   978-1-84262-765-5 pbk

First published in Great Britain in 2008 by The Book Guild Ltd.

Copyright © Melanie Whitehouse 2008

Cover illustration © Arcangel Images

Published in Large Print 2010 by arrangement with
Book Guild Publishing

Dales Large Print is an imprint of Library Magna Books Ltd.

Printed and bound in Great Britain by
T.J. (International) Ltd., Cornwall, PL28 8RW

Dedicated to all the wonderful cats and dogs I've already met and all those I've yet to meet, and in particular to the real Augustus Moon and Tosca. You are simply the best.

Chapter One

Spying

I've been watching her. She doesn't know it but I have. Every day I creep up the long, dark alley between the two houses and hide in the dense rhododendron bushes at the back of the garden. It's the perfect spot for sussing out her movements. I want to know who comes and goes, whether she has a man in her life and if she has children and a dog. Once I have that information, I will make my decision.

So far, it's looking good. She appears to live in the little white cottage on her own and she seems to be there most of the day and in most nights watching the television. On fine days she spends lunchtime in her garden but she's never seen me hidden behind the trellis, watching, watching, watching with my grape-green eyes.

It's now the end of the summer and I need to find a place to rest my bones before winter comes. I have been homeless for too long.

Living rough and scrounging scraps from the woods and fields is all very well when you're a youngster but I'm middle-aged now.

It wasn't my fault I lost the place I'd always called home. I'd lived there all my life with my mother and sister but then they moved house and, due to circumstances that spiralled out of my control, I got left behind. It was impossible for me to make the journey 200 miles north east on my own so I stayed on, in the only place I've ever known. But now there are new people in my house and I'm not welcome any more.

So, I've been forced to roam the streets at night, foraging in bins for food, and hiding away during the day in secret corners in case someone spots me and my shame becomes the talk of the village. What will become of me? I don't know ... but she is my last hope. Tonight's the night. I'm going to pop in and introduce myself. I wonder if she'll like me? My whole future depends on what happens this evening.

Success! I waited in the alley until I knew she was in the garden and then I made my move. She had friends around and I was hoping that even if she wasn't too pleased to see me, they would at least talk to me. As I sauntered in through the back gate, I heard a loud bang which I know usually means champagne and celebrations. It turns out it was her birthday and she was having a bit of a party. Everyone seemed delighted to see me and I spoke to them all in turn, telling them a little of my story but not enough to make them feel sorry for me. I'm too proud to seek pity.

I heard one say, 'My God, he's a handsome beast,' and another, 'I always go for the slim, dark types like him,' so I knew I'd made a good impression. Then I made my excuses and left. I felt quite sad to leave such a merry bunch but I knew it was for the best. I shall pay a return visit soon. Meanwhile, I'll keep watching her from the secret seclusion of the trees at the back of the garden.

Tonight I went round again and this time I told her my story, the whole sorry tale from start to finish. I stood by the back door and gazed straight at her. I didn't take my eyes off her for a second as I explained what had happened and how I felt about everything. She seemed most sympathetic, exclaiming every now and again, 'Oh, you poor thing!' or 'How awful for you.' It was exactly the result I'd hoped for. Then I said my goodbyes. I think my future is assured but I don't want to rush things so I shall come back tomorrow to seal it. Softly softly catchee woman.

She was sitting alone on the sofa when I strolled in through the living room door the next night. She looked at me – and I stared back. This was the moment I'd been building up to. Would she go for it? 'Why don't you come and sit here?' she said, patting the space beside her. I obeyed. It felt so good to sit on something comfortable again. Tentatively, I reached out and patted her hand. She leaned over and scratched me behind the ears.

You see, I am a cat.

Chapter Two

The Mistress's Tale

It was 10 o'clock on a sunny August morning and Maisie Maddox was at her bedroom window, peering into a tiny mirror perched on the sill, searching for non-existent spots to squeeze. As a freelance journalist who worked from home it was something she did whenever she was stuck for words and today inspiration had failed her. Again. As had the spots. Her skin had cleared up since she'd moved out of Brighton's polluted air and it was playing havoc with her work.

'What is there to be inspired about?' she muttered. 'Another skinny celebrity, Botoxed to the eyeballs, talking through stiff lips about their battle with their weight, pretending they haven't had plastic surgery despite their permanently startled look, and refusing to give you anything interesting to put in your article.'

Maisie sighed. It went against the grain to admit it but she was bored and a bit lonely.

She loved her pretty little white cottage, she loved the ancient East Sussex village of Cuckstone, the rolling South Downs and the lush countryside studded with oak and beech trees but she didn't like the isolation. It had been a brave shot in the dark, moving to a place where she knew nobody, and it was taking a while to break into the cliques which made up village life. Some of the women she'd met since she moved here didn't work for a living at all, yet they seemed busier than the friends she'd left behind in Brighton who worked flat out and who she hardly saw from one month's end to the next. Even so, they were, on the whole, a welcoming crowd and she'd begun to make some new friends and be invited out. There always seemed to be someone cranking up a barbecue or inviting her for drinks and she hoped that before too long she'd know enough people to be able to throw her own party.

Life in Cuckstone was much more integrated than the rather lonely one she remembered from her childhood. Maisie had grown up in the country on the other side of Sussex, the eldest of three girls who spent their childhood running wild, usually in pursuit of a pack of disobedient, hungry basset hounds intent on stealing some poor family's picnic. Country life as she recalled it was harsh but wholesome. Indelibly etched in her mind were scenes of icy winters, where her mum's bras and dad's Y-fronts froze solid on the washing line, taking on a disembodied look, as if the person was still inside them, flattened and invisible. Poking the frozen garments into naughty shapes as they melted in front of the Rayburn had amused her and her younger sisters Mandy and Millie for hours. Winters were real winters then. Vast icicles had dripped off the house for weeks, huge drifts of snow had fallen, and the unmade-up drive would freeze and leave the family stranded, despite her mum putting hot ashes on it every morning. There was always a stinky, rusting paraffin heater wheezing away in the loo overnight to stop the pan freezing up, and intricate Jack Frost patterns would decorate the inside of the windows in the mornings.

Then there were the summers ... picnics on the South Downs and in the garden, eating sun-warmed strawberries and raspberries, swimming in rivers and friends' pools, days out riding on borrowed ponies. The long, light evenings were spent running around the nearby common building camps, then falling asleep exhausted in a tent in the garden to be woken as the sun came up by the loudest dawn chorus Maisie had ever heard. Their garden had been a haven for wildlife and in the autumn, fairy-rings of mushrooms bloomed under the apple trees. It was a magical place and when Maisie's parents had had to leave it due to her dad's ill health, it had broken her heart.

Most fondly of all from her childhood, though, Maisie remembered their gang of bassets: Diggy, so-called because she decided to dig to Australia under the hydrangea bush during one particularly bad-tempered phantom pregnancy; and her daughters Sophie (after Sophia Loren because she was so incredibly beautiful with her high-domed head) and runt-of-the-litter Vicky Voo, or, to give her her full name, Victoria Plum Spinster (because she'd never been had and was therefore a spinster of the parish).

Voo was Maisie's own dog, the only animal she'd ever owned. Maisie had been overjoyed when she'd been given Voo's pedigree certificate on her 12th birthday – a bit of a misleading document, given that Voo was never going to be shown anywhere as she had one blue eye and one brown, but then that was what Maisie had loved about her. In the dark, the lens of Voo's blue eye glowed like a ruby and her brown eye like a sapphire. In fact she was a jewel of a dog for a lonely teenager and had lived a long and happy life, only dying after Maisie had completed her training as a journalist in Plymouth and moved to London to try her luck in Fleet Street.

She had been a freelance feature writer for years now but it had been extremely tricky at times. When mortgage payments went up, she had more than once thought she would lose the home she'd spent so much time and money renovating, but she always managed to hang on to it by writing extra articles. As someone who loved art and making a place look beautiful, she'd invested her savings in an interior design course, which in turn had led to her working on the monthly glossies. That had led to her becoming an editor for a company in London – the best freelance job she'd ever had and the one she was doing now. It brought in a regular, if small, monthly income and enabled her to fit other work around it. But it also meant she had to interview celebrities – one of her least favourite tasks as so many of them, with a few fabulous exceptions, refused to play ball.

Now, if only I could write about animals

all the time, thought Maisie. They wouldn't want copy approval or complain that it wasn't a glowing feature. The bassets would make a good subject for a start...

At that point, Maisie's phone rang. It was Trisha, the commissioning editor of a monthly magazine and one of the few Maisie both respected and liked.

'I want an article on a woman who moves to the country,' she said. 'You'll need to talk about your fabulous new life there and how you've met the locals, any talent in the village, how you spend your time ... I don't need to tell you, you know the score, but we need the copy this afternoon, we're running late.'

As always, thought Maisie, but didn't say it. At least it shouldn't take too long to write. The only problem is that I'm not actually enjoying my life here yet. I'll have to wing it a bit.

She recalled a phrase that a friend of hers on a Sunday newspaper used regularly. 'Sprinkle it with stardust,' he'd say. What he meant was, 'Flam it up, go as far as you can without getting us sued.' There was going to have to be a large helping of stardust in this article.

'I know, I'll write about how I am at last

going to get a dog now I've become a bumpkin,' she said to Trisha. 'I'll write about how a dog is for extroverts because it takes you outdoors and helps you meet people, and a cat is for introverts, because you can't take a cat anywhere. Anyway, I don't like cats. They're stuck up and snooty, you can't take them for walks and get fit and they catch mice and birds. A cat is SO not for me.'

As Maisie sat at her computer, the idea took shape. In fact the more she thought about it the more real it became and the more that reality appealed.

'I have a fantasy basset hound puppy in my head and she's even got a name. She's called Myrtle,' typed Maisie. 'It seems to sum up that sad basset face so perfectly, those huge paddy paws, melancholy eyes and long, silky, droopy ears.

'A dog might even help me to meet a man. It has been a long time since I've had a relationship that's had any glimmer of hope to it.'

Maisie stopped typing. Her romantic life had not been what she'd hoped for and now, at 46, there really wasn't much hope of having children. People said you got over that but she didn't believe it. If you'd always wanted children, then you didn't just put it behind you. You pretended you had but it carried itself with you wherever you went. Of course there was still time – if the right man came into her life this very second and probably involving IVF. But without that combination, she had to face the fact that kids just weren't going to happen and she didn't know if she would ever get over it. When she thought about it, which was often, she felt as if she was in mourning for something she'd lost because she had always believed she would have kids – it was as much of a certainty as the fact that she was a woman. In her mind, she'd realised quite recently, she had taken it for granted that she would grow up, have a good job and work hard, find a nice man, get married, move to the country and live in a modest-sized old house (a Georgian rectory would do fine), give up work, have children (no set number) and bring them up making jam and chutneys from local produce and walking the dogs every day.

Deep down, Maisie felt she was largely to blame for what she viewed as her total failure with men. 'You're just a bad picker,' her old schoolfriend Fi had said once, and it was true. Mind you, Fi wasn't that great a picker either – her husband was the archetypal chinless wonder with a stuck-up public school attitude to match, and their marriage had run its course long ago. But the men had been there for the taking once. Where had they all gone now? It was as if there had been a Man Bank, open all hours and offering a wide variety of products to suit every female, until she was about 35. Then it had suddenly changed hands, the victim of a buy-out by women who'd got there before her and had handpicked the best deals. All that was left was dross and damaged goods but she still lived in hope that one day she would bag a bargain basement bloke who turned out to be priceless.

Maisie allowed her mind to roam back in time – not somewhere it was often given permission to go as it perennially got lodged on one particular man. Mike. The married one. The one she could never have had because he was already committed to his wife and two young children but the one she had loved above all others. When they'd met she hadn't been looking for a relationship but was concentrating on her career and try-ing to make a name for herself as a feature writer. Mike worked in television as a pro-ducer and they had met when she'd been sent by a national newspaper to cover the launch of a new programme. It was New Year's Day and she had such a terrible hangover that she couldn't find the words to ask him a single question about his documentary. After he'd finished the press conference he came over to enquire whether she was all right because, in his words, she looked 'a bit peaky'.

She'd explained about overdoing the booze to get through a very tedious dinner party on New Year's Eve. They had discussed how whatever you did on December 31st it was always a letdown, and he'd invited her for a coffee. Mike was tall and slim with crinkly blond hair and unusually deep and compassionate brown eyes that seemed to cut through her toxic gloom. He was, she found, lively and funny with a sharp wit that matched her own and by the time she'd finished her skinny cappuccino she found herself suggesting she interview him the following week about his documentary. It was, of course, a ruse so that she could see him again and they both knew it, but this was an affair that seemed destined to happen, no matter what.

Even though it took a couple of months to get started, during which he'd spent three weeks away with his family on holiday, it somehow felt so right – and yet, of course, it wasn't, it was so wrong. Maisie knew that all along and she acknowledged that everyone involved would get hurt, but no matter how often she brought this up and discussed it with Mike, they couldn't give each other up. She felt caught up in the grip of a love that was more powerful than anything she'd experienced before and he treated her so much better than any of the single men she'd been out with. He rang when he said he would, turned up on time, listened to her struggles to establish herself as a freelance journalist and advised her when she got stuck with a feature. He was quite nostalgic and soppy, too – he gave her presents on the anniversaries of little things, such as when they first met, when they first kissed and the first time they went to bed together... As well as the love, though, they had also had respect for each other and that was something she'd never found again with any other man.

Then, after two years together, Mike's wife had found out about their affair and Mike had, as Maisie always knew he would, stayed with her and the children. Maisie knew if she'd been the one with kids, she'd have stayed and she knew he was right to do so but at the time – 13 years ago now – she thought she'd actually die of the pain. She couldn't understand why it hurt so much physically when it was her heart that had been mortally wounded. The only way through it had been to drink herself into oblivion one night and then have to go to work and spend the entire next day concentrating on not throwing up into her wastepaper bin or over her desk. Then the day after she'd get rabidly drunk again. She still had a hole in her shin where she'd walked into a metal trunk one night after downing half a bottle of Scotch.

They didn't so much split up as drift apart but, while the pain subsided after a few months and dulled to an ache that she learned to live with, their affair had always felt unresolved because, she supposed, their passion had been severed at its height. She felt there was nowhere to put that great flaming orb of love that she had for him and although it shrank to a tight, black ball in her heart over the years, its core still smouldered sporadically.

Unlike some of her friends, who moved from boyfriend to boyfriend until they found the one they settled down with, her heart didn't seem to recover with the years.

Although she tried, she simply couldn't fall in love with Jim, the kind, sweet, lovely man she met the following year, because her heart was still shackled to her ex-lover. Then Slippery Sid, who she met a couple of years later, wooed her, won her – and dumped her from a great height after she told him she loved him. No matter that he'd said it to her a dozen times – she realised in retrospect he had always said it down the phone and never to her face.

The next insignificant other had been Rampant Rob. She'd gone out with him for six months but he was younger than her and looking back, it had been fairly obvious that he hadn't wanted a relationship. Basically a nice but weak man, he couldn't see a way out of it so he kept stringing her along. Maisie and Rob worked for the same magazine at the time and he had probably thought she would blacken his name if he dumped her. A last-minute shag on a Saturday night if he'd finished his game of football, had had a drink with the lads and had nothing better to do was all he was good for, yet she'd allowed herself to be treated badly by him for all that time because she was desperate to make it work, desperate to get pregnant before it was too late. And although she hadn't really wanted a child without being married, time was running out, so she'd taken the odd risk and it still hadn't happened.

Thus the man fiasco continued, with the Man Bank running increasingly dry and refusing to give her any credit at all in the last couple of years. But a dog ... think of Pongo and Missus and how they brought their owners together. She knew other examples – David and Natasha, who met in a park while walking their dogs and had never been apart since, sharing their space with three Weimeraners and two smelly German pointers. Maybe she should pursue her Myrtle. But she would have to be for the future, not the present, because Maisie had work to do on her two-bedroom cottage before she could have any animal. The kitchen was a ramshackle affair tacked on the back of the house. It went off at a slant, so that the wall narrowed to just five feet at one end. There was a plinth here, apparently the remains of the outside loo which had been resited upstairs in a bathroom built above the alleyway between the two houses.

No, the kitchen had to be done before she could think about getting a dog, and it was a major task. The whole structure had to be demolished and rebuilt so that it was safe, secure and much, much bigger. It would take all Maisie's money and work was due to begin in a few months' time.

'I can't even go and look for my Myrtle puppy, who I intend to buy from a rescue centre, until I have the kitchen rebuilt, so I'm stuck here on my own until that happens,' concluded Maisie's feature. 'Then, with the building completed, I shall share my home with a dog for the first time in my adult life. I'm sure it will transform my life – and I can't wait!'

Maisie filed her copy and, with thoughts of Myrtle in her head, she wandered into the garden. There seemed to be a commotion coming from up the road. Lots of shouting was going on, engines were revving and drivers were swearing. This really is a rat-run, she thought wearily, glancing at a removal van parked a few doors away and clearly the cause of the rumpus. If I'd only known the people who used this narrow little B-road were so foul-tempered and impatient, maybe I'd have found somewhere else to move to. And if I do get a puppy I'll be terrified of letting her run free. What if she should run on to the road? She'd be squashed in an instant.

At that moment a man appeared from up

the road. 'You haven't seen my cat, have you?' he asked. 'Black with green eyes, long and lean, baggy stomach. Called Blackie... He's escaped from his cat basket and I'm just about to move house and can't leave without him.'

'No, sorry, I've been indoors all day working,' said Maisie, thinking that had to be the world's most unimaginative name for a cat. 'I'll keep an eye out for him.'

She went into the kitchen, made herself a Marmite and peanut butter sandwich and strolled out to her back garden. It was only small but surrounded by a flint and brick wall and filled with rambling roses, honeysuckle and other pretty, cottage garden plants.

There on the wall was a black cat with the most opalescent green eyes she'd ever seen and he was staring at her. He looked terrified.

'Here, kitty kitty,' she said, walking towards him but he bolted under the garden shed. She'd never been any good with cats. At that moment his owner appeared at the back gate. 'Have you seen him? I think he came this way.'

'Yes, he's under the shed,' said Maisie. 'Come in and grab him if you like.'

At that point Blackie the cat made a bolt for next door's garden, his owner grabbed him by the back legs – and the cat turned and scratched him on his forearm. Blood beaded from the cuts as the man yelped with pain and let go of the cat, who leapt onto the wall and over the other side.

Maisie wrapped a paper towel round the man's arm as he cursed. 'I'm going to have to leave him behind,' he said. 'Shame, he's a good cat. I'll ask my neighbour to leave some food out for him.'

Over the next week Maisie didn't see any sign of the cat and assumed he had either been found by his owner and taken to pastures new or had moved in with somebody else. Even so, she didn't like to think of him going hungry if he was still around, so every night she'd toast a fishfinger (Maisie's favourite hangover cure was Slut's Delight – a fishfinger cooked for speed in the toaster and served in a sandwich with butter, black pepper and tomato ketchup) and leave it out on an old saucer for him in the garden. Each morning it was gone, though there was still no sign of the cat.

A fortnight later it was her 46th birthday and a sweltering summer's night. A few old friends had come over for a barbecue and everyone was sitting in the garden drinking Maisie's Raspberry Rockets – a divine but lethal concoction of pink champagne, raspberry vodka and creme de framboise topped up with cranberry and raspberry juice – when there was a quiet miaow from the garden gate. It was the black cat. After sizing up the situation he moved over to wind around the legs of her friends. Then he came up to Maisie.

'You're being adopted,' said her friend Lucy, who lived a couple of miles away on the edge of Cuckstone.

'You're joking, I don't want a cat,' said Maisie.

Lucy laughed. 'I know cats and I'm telling you he wants you. You won't have a say in it.'

Maisie thought no more of it but the next night, as she stood by her back door, the cat appeared again. 'Miaow,' he said loudly, looking at her with his slanting green eyes.

'Miaow to you, too,' she said.

'Miaaaaow,' he replied, fixing her in his gaze. And he just kept on staring at her and miaowing, each one louder and longer than the last. It was quite extraordinary. Maisie couldn't help feeling the cat was telling her his story, and a sorry tale it was, too, one of desertion and abandonment, of being misunderstood and left to starve. And there was a need there, a desperate need for something. Then just as suddenly as he'd started miaowing he stopped, turned on his black velvet heel and stalked off.

What was all that about? Maisie wondered. She was soon to find out.

The next night, as she watched John Nettles (who she'd fancied madly since his leaner *Bergerac* days) in *Midsomer Murders*, she heard a tiny "ow?' It was the black cat. She patted the sofa next to her and to her surprise he jumped up and with a big sigh flopped down a few inches from where she sat. Tentatively she put out a hand to him and laid it next to him on the couch. Very carefully he extended one ebony paw and with his claws at full stretch, very gently put them into her hand and pulled it towards him. She realised he wanted to be stroked.

'Poor boy, you've been deprived of affection for weeks and you're desperate for love, aren't you?' said Maisie, caressing the top of his head. And as she gazed into his green eyes and gently stroked his dusty fur, her dog-loving heart was lost.

PAWNOTE: So she fell for it and here I am, about to live in luxury again. In the end it was so simple. All I had to do was turn up a few times, tell her my sorry tale and miaow my way into her life. Oh yes, and put my paw out and touch her hand. That always worked a treat when I was living with my previous owners. Even that time I scratched the new stair runner to pieces within a week of it being laid (it was their fault for leaving me and my sister alone while they went on holiday. I was bored and everybody knows that a carpet with a looped pile feels too good on the claws to be ignored). But I was forgiven after I patted my mistress's hand with my paw. It took a few days to wheedle *him* round but I got there in the end. It's a winsome trick that I learned from my mother and it works on humans without fail.

Of course there are many things my new mistress needs to learn and it will be my duty to teach her over the coming months, for if everything pans out as planned I intend to stay here for a long time. The rest of my life, in fact.

The most important thing for me, after all those weeks spent living rough, is to find a comfy bed to sleep in. I like to seek out various places to rest around a house. It doesn't do to be too predictable, you don't need a human knowing where you are at any given time. No, my advice to other cats is to line up a selection of beds and rotate, in no set order. Include wardrobes and a couple of high spots, such as the top of a kitchen cupboard. If you want them to know you are there, miaow at them – they're usually impressed that you've climbed into such an ingenious place. Also, if humans change things – and they seem to be obsessed with moving furniture around every so often, I can't understand why – you will always have another safe, soft spot to rest your paws.

In her house there are two big beds upstairs and both seem a likely place for a cat like me to make my own. In the back bedroom I will get the morning sun, in the front bedroom the evening sun. Of course, she won't be used to sharing a bed with me but persistence usually pays off. I shall jump on her at night if not. What person could resist the lure of stroking my soft fur before they drop off to sleep? No, when she goes to bed – and I suspect that is later than I would like, so I shall have to sort that out, too – I expect affection. I will curl up by her side for 10 minutes, so she can tickle me behind the ears and stroke my head soothingly. But the thing she must never do and to which I will always object vocally and voraciously is to pick me up. I am not a lap cat – never have been, never will be. I refuse to be treated as if I were a teddy bear, although I hear other, lesser breeds like it. I am a proud beast – I like to think I look a little like a panther with my sleek dark fur, mesmeric eyes and long, elegant tail. OK, I'm not in the best shape at the moment but within a few weeks and with some decent food and lots of uninterrupted rest I will be as regal and alluring as ever I was.

There are a number of places around the house where I intend to stake my claim but expect to meet resistance. The dining table, for instance. I can predict that I will be ignominiously turfed off a few times and the words 'unhygienic' and 'dirty footprints' will be muttered but in the end I will break her down. It is, after all, the perfect spot from which to watch the garden and see who comes and goes. I need to do a lot of surveillance work before I can step into the back garden and be confident that no intruders are waiting for me.

Then there is food – she clearly needs to be educated on that score. I expect fresh meat and fish on a regular basis but I'm not that impressed by what she's served up so far. Cold fishfingers with burned bits on the outside? What does she think I am? And supermarket own-brand catfood? It may be from Waitrose but even so. Does she think I look like a cat that eats that muck? No, I like top-grade stuff and in particular the one that comes in the little sparkly tin. I can spot it a mile off but it doesn't come my way often. I need to teach her my ways if I'm to be happy living here.

I do, of course, get up early in the morning and expect to be fed as soon as I'm awake. In summer that can be any time from 5am onwards. In winter it is later – I'm a cat that reacts to the daylight and in winter I can be very, very slothful indeed. In fact I've heard humans talking about SAD syndrome and I think I, too, suffer from Seasonal Affective Disorder. There's nothing to do at that time of year – there are no mice hanging around the nearby allotments, so there's nothing to catch and bring in to contribute to the larder. In summer I will bring her lots of presents, as I get the feeling she's not much good at hunting for herself.

Most important of all, though, is that she remains on her own. I shall get rid of other males, by fair means or foul. I cannot warn her but she will find out.

Chapter Three

A Working Relationship

At 5am precisely, Maisie was fast asleep, snoring gently, in the back bedroom. She always denied she snored but friends who had stayed told her otherwise these days. She put it down to two things: she'd put on a bit of weight over the years, which apparently played havoc with the airways at night, and both her parents had snored like human thunderclaps. During her childhood, she had regularly played a game with her sisters to work out which snore belonged to which parent. Either way, their mum and dad had spent 40 years of marriage blaming the other for keeping him or her awake. There's something to be said for staying single, Maisie had often thought, and loud snoring is up at the top of the list.

She liked this bedroom in summer because it was quiet and looked out over the back garden instead of facing the aggressive road at the front. But right now she wasn't thinking of anything, just drifting around in a happy dream. The pale blue curtains embroidered with wild flowers fluttered in the faint breeze that washed over her as she slept through the sultry August night. She looked so peaceful – until she was woken up by something heavy and solid landing right on top of her stomach.

'Phooofff,' said Maisie, the wind knocked out of her. She opened her eyes to see a pair of luminous green orbs fixed on her face in the dim, dawn light.

'You rotten little sod,' she said. 'What do you want?' She took a quick look at Blackie's feet. Were his paws really made of concrete? Surely he couldn't catch birds and mice if that's how he went about it. No, he'd clearly meant to wake her up, so that must mean he wanted something.

'Miaow,' he went loudly.

'What do you want?' she said. 'I fed you last night, you can't want to eat again.'

The miaows continued. Maisie got up, shooed the cat off the bed and shut the door. As it had never closed properly and she was useless at DIY, she barricaded it with a large box. Then she crawled back into bed and settled down to sleep again. As she nodded off she could hear the box being pushed across the floor as the cat shoved from the other side. Then... 'Phoooff'. He'd landed on her again and was miaowing again.

'Why are you doing this?' she cried in exasperation. 'I have to work to earn your catfood and you keep waking me up. You're an ungrateful tyke.'

Maisie gave it a third go but soon realised that the cat was going to give her no peace. She went downstairs and filled a bowl full of tuna – human-grade tuna, there was nothing else in the cupboard that she could give him. Today, she thought, I have to go shopping for him. I have to buy a basket, wet food, dry food, worm pills and God knows what else. He's going to cost me a fortune. And how the hell do I get a worm pill down him on my own? He must have worms, he's been living rough for weeks, and he'll need treating.

The cat tucked into the tuna, clearing his bowl in seconds. 'Boy, you were hungry,' said Maisie. Even she couldn't eat that fast and she loved her food. Licking his lips the cat looked at her appreciatively. 'You're very beautiful,' she said as she made a cup of tea. 'Do you want to come upstairs for a cuddle?' He followed her back to the bedroom and curled up on the other side of the bed, watching her warily before his eyes closed.

Maisie drifted off and woke up at the more reasonable hour of 7.30 to find the cat gazing at her, as if he was trying to imprint her face on his memory. I wonder if he will be able to remember my face once he gets to know me, she thought. But how will I tell him from any other black cat in the area? Apart from his long, slim tail and his eyes – which in this light are a greeny grey, like a mountain stream over pebbles – he's just another common or garden moggy.

At that point, Blackie stretched himself and as he stretched he got longer – and longer – and longer. Maisie was amazed. The baggy skin under his tummy suddenly made sense. Was this animal made of some kind of special cat-elastic? Maybe that's what cat gut was. With his paws out in front and his body stretched out behind, he went on for ever. 'You are *so* long,' she said. 'You must be at least four feet from your claws to the tip of your tail.' The sun's rays hit the east-facing room at that point and lit up the cat's fur. He wasn't actually black, she saw, more of a rippling dark chocolate with black lowlights and some subtle, deep auburn highlights where the hot summer sun had bleached his fur. It was a look any supermodel would die for, thought Maisie enviously, twirling her own highlighted and very wayward blonde hair. There would be no bad hair days for that cat.

Sitting there in the early morning sunlight he was extremely handsome, in fact – and he looked as if he knew it, though his coat was rather neglected. 'You need to give yourself a good wash, mate,' she told him. 'Spruce yourself up a bit and you'll be the best looking lad in the village.' She tickled him behind the ears and he purred – and the more she tickled, the louder his purr became.

'Enough,' she said. 'You'll turn me into a time waster.' He jumped off the bed and went to sit on the stairs, where he kept watch until Maisie came out of the bathroom. As she stepped over his tail, which was twitching dementedly, she looked into his eyes. She could swear he narrowed them slightly before blinking, slowly. It was a look of love, something she'd never seen before in a cat. Dogs, of course, you could see them loving you almost every minute they were with you, but a cat? Don't be daft, she told herself, they're too independent. But he continued to look at her as if he was grateful for having been taken in and looked after.

'Miaaaow,' he chirrupped.

Maisie was moved. 'I shall make you a pledge, not-so-little cat,' she said. 'I promise to look after you to the end of your days. You need never worry again about having enough food or being cold in winter. This is your home now and I am your new mistress. But we shall have to think of a new name for you. I'm not calling you Blackie, you're so beautiful that you're worth something far more imaginative than that.'

She thought for a moment. 'You came to me on a moonlit August night,' she said. 'I shall call you Augustus Moon – Gus for short. What do you think of your new name, Gus? Do you like it?' The cat chirruped again, got up, stretched one leg in the air like a ballet dancer at the barre and started to groom. Maybe he'd been suffering from low self-esteem and needed the love of a good woman to get his act together. 'Good boy,' said Maisie. 'Give yourself a clean-up, you know you're worth it.'

Maisie made her breakfast and wrote a shopping list for Gus, then went to the nearest town to load up. First stop the pet shop, where she bought him a sheepskin hammock basket. He'll love that, slung over the radiator, all snug and warm in the winter, she thought. Then she bought worm pills, flea spray, a stretchy purple velvet collar with a bell to warn the birds he was coming and a squeaky mouse filled with catnip. He'll be well pleased, she thought.

Next she went to the supermarket and bought him a big bag of dry biscuits and two large packets of cat food – different brands, just in case he was anti one of them. You never knew with cats, apparently they were fussy creatures. In total he'd cost her an eye-watering £47.95 – not a good thing at the end of a not very lucrative month but what the heck. That's what credit cards were for.

On returning home, Maisie spent a frus-trating couple of hours trying to work out how to put the sheepskin hammock together. It seemed to want to work in a back-to-front way and however she twisted the arms it would not fit together in any logical pattern. But then DIY never had anything to do with logic, thought Maisie grimly, recalling the time she'd put together an entire Ikea Billy bookcase back to front. You needed the sort of brain that did the cryptic crossword to sort out flat-pack instructions and hers was only capable of tackling the quick crossword. Still, this was just a cat basket, not a piece of Ikea flat-pack with a name like Git or Arstid – such apt names, she'd decided long ago.

After struggling for a couple of hours, the air blue with swear words that would make a navvy blush, she gave in and took the sheep-skin hammock back to the shop in a filthy temper. 'It must be faulty,' she said to the assistant. One twist later and he'd handed it back to her looking just like a cat basket.

'Not faulty in the slightest, you just have to know what to do,' he winked.

'Huh. Well, thank you,' said Maisie. She was a great believer in good manners and, having been well brought-up, would auto-matically say please or thank you however short-tempered she was feeling. In fact, she thought as she drove home, mentally cata-loguing the sullen teenagers, screaming kids, arrogant parking wardens, bad drivers, rude drivers and drivers of any oversized four-wheel drive vehicle who made her grumpy, good manners really do count.

At that point a car pulled out in front of her. 'You silly cow,' she yelled, sticking two fingers up through the sun roof. At least she would have done had she not forgotten to open the sun roof. 'Yow!' she cried, sucking her fingers. The driver of the other car gave her a perfectly straight, one-finger salute in victorious response.

By the time Maisie had driven home the pain in her hand had faded to a dull throb. Proudly she slipped the fleece cover over the cat's basket and slung the basket over the radiator. He was hanging around watching her.

'Come on then, jump up,' she said. 'Give it a go, this has taken me ages and almost cost me two fingers.' He looked at her as if she was mad and jumped on the dining table. 'Get off there,' yelled Maisie. She picked him up and as he struggled – he clearly hated being picked up and stuck all four paws out stiffly like a cartoon cat – she put him gently into the new cat basket. He jumped out again and bolted for the door, disappearing for the rest of the day. 'There's no pleasing some cats,' said Maisie.

After an entire week of trying and failing to entice him to use his expensive hammock she gave up, removed the sheepskin cover and put it over a chair. Immediately he jumped onto it and settled down. He obviously doesn't like wobbly things, she concluded. But he'd also avoided the catnip mouse, jumping whenever it squeaked, and had refused to eat some of the cat food, which spent the day festering in the dish collecting flies' eggs. She'd had no chance of getting him to wear his velvet collar, either, because he scarpered the second she went near him with it. He was definitely a very awkward animal indeed, Maisie decided. Or was he proving a point? Was he trying to establish himself as boss-cat round here?

By this time, however, there were more pressing things on her mind and in particularly the sensitive issue of fleas. He had them for sure – she'd seen them jumping on the stair carpet and had bites on her leg to prove it – but getting the flea spray onto him was impossible. She'd go to grab him but he would slither out of her arms and run away to hide under a cupboard or in the garden. Why was he always one step ahead of her? Maisie wondered. Could he read her body language? Maybe she was giving the game away by looking furtive. She'd never been much good at concealing her thoughts. Her mouth might come out with acquiescent and polite words to editors but she'd realised early on in her working life that her face showed that she was simultaneously calling him or her every name under the sun, clear as day.

She also needed to worm Gus but, in spite of trying every trick in the book – crushing

up worm tablets in strong-smelling pilchards in tomato sauce, disguising the pill in
a piece of stinky cheese, trying to prise open
his jaws to slip a pill down his throat – she'd
failed. A visit to a vet was in order, she
decided, but without the cat.

Maisie had always been good at tracking
people down and it occurred to her that
Gus would probably have been treated by a
local vet in the past. As she already knew
where he used to live it shouldn't be too
complicated.

As she was on the way to the vet's her
mobile rang. 'It's Mags, calling for a chat,'
screeched an Australian voice. 'Whatcha
doin', mate?'

'Hi Mags, I'm just going to the vet's,'
replied Maisie.

'The vet's?' said Mags. 'What's the matter
with you? Can't you go to the doctor like
any normal person?'

Maisie and Mags had met on holiday in
Bangkok many years before and had laughed
most of the way to Bali together before Mags
had settled in Australia and got married to a
bad lot who she later divorced. Maisie would
never forget one particular occasion when
Mags – deprived of alcohol all through
Malaysia because she couldn't bear beer and

48

that was the only drink available – had got hold of a bottle of vodka. They were in Java, in the cultural capital, Yogyakarta, and due to go out for a meal, so Mags had secreted the Smirnoff in her biggest bag, told Maisie what she was up to and they'd agreed to order orange juice all night in the teetotal restaurant (it was a Muslim country, after all) where they were going for a meal. Which they did, the orange juice getting increasingly weaker, the vodka stronger and Maisie and Mags more and more drunk. The night ended when Maisie potted every ball on the pool table onto the floor and collapsed into a tri-shaw where she made a total fool of herself by making a pass at their English guide.

Maisie explained to Mags she'd got a cat – or rather, that a cat had got her.

'Thoughtcha liked dogs, mate,' said Mags. 'Didn't you want a basset called Mortal or some such thing?'

'Myrtle, you dingo,' replied Maisie. 'I'm going to get a dog later. For now the cat has adopted me and I've promised to look after him.'

Mags rang off but not until she'd called Maisie a soft touch. It was true, Maisie knew she was soppy. She was sentimental, nostalgic, over-indulgent and at times greedy but she had a kind heart and she was a good cook. She loved nothing more than to entertain friends but that usually involved eating too much, a habit which was her downfall. She viewed food as a friend that was forever there for you and never let you down. The trouble was that while Maisie had read enough self-help books to know that her body was supposed to be a temple, she also knew she'd made it too many offerings over the years, which was why her curves seemed to go in every direction these days. It served her right, really. She'd once told her youngest sister Millie that her legs were like tree trunks, one of which should be felled, so it was only right and just that she'd ended up porky, too. Still, Millie had soon got her own back as they drove past the mushroom factory which perpetually stank of the fishmeal they used as a fertiliser. 'Close your legs, Maisie,' Millie had roared. Their mother had almost crashed the car she'd laughed so much. Maisie hadn't been amused.

As she pondered the horror of joining WeightWatchers for the umpteenth time, she arrived at the vet's and explained her predicament.

'No problem, if he was brought in here we

should have his details on our computer,' said the helpful receptionist. 'Oh yes, here he is ... he's half Burmese – mother pure-bred Burmese, father unknown but thought to be a local farm cat, possibly feral. Burmese are the dog-end of the cat spectrum, you know. They're often quite nervy and territorial but can be dog-like in their devotion.

'Health-wise, he was once scratched badly on his flank through fighting, he has been neutered and is due to be wormed – he has a pill once a year but it's a devil to get down him. He also has a sister who was badly injured as a kitten when she was knocked down by a car, and he's six years old in October. I don't have an actual date.'

Maisie was amazed. That meant she could give him a birthday and the obvious one for a black cat with green eyes living with a single woman was Hallowe'en. What could be more perfect? Just as long as the locals didn't bring back the witches' ducking stool.

The vet's assistant gave her a special capsule which had to be trickled onto the back of an animal's neck to treat fleas and one kind of worms. The other worms, whatever they were and however wriggly, would have to wait. These treatments cost another

£15 and Maisie's funds were exhausted.

So, too, was she, once she'd tried to apply the liquid to Gus. You need three hands, she thought. One to hold him by the neck, one to take the top off the capsule and a third to get it through his thick pelt onto the skin of his neck. What a palaver! Half of the stuff – which smelled acridly of chemicals – went all over his fur before he wrenched free and ran off, turning to gaze at her with mal-evolence as he reached the back wall. If looks could kill, thought Maisie, I'd just have been turned to stone.

Getting used to living harmoniously with a mature animal was not that easy, she reflected. There was a huge learning curve on both sides and he probably wasn't finding it straightforward, either. After a week of interrupted nights when she had been pounced on at dawn, Maisie had come to the conclusion that his previous owners fed him at 6am and had reluctantly given in. Now she took a bowl of cat food up to bed every night and left it for him on the landing. It stank in this hot weather but it had put paid to the pouncing and bouncing that had been going on and interrupting her beauty sleep. Her friends were already saying she'd been wound round his little paw and they were right. Each night at around 10.30pm he made it visibly plain that it was high time she came up to bed. If she had friends round he'd prowl into the sitting room and jump on the sofa or sit on the back of the armchair glaring at her but he wouldn't settle down until she turned the lights off and carried his dish of cat food upstairs.

Maisie thought it was rather sweet. He obviously liked his night-time cuddle when he settled down on her bed and nuzzled into the crook of her arm. She didn't like it quite so much when she turned off the light and he began to groom. Lick, lick, lick, he went, slurp, slurp, slurp, one befurred leg high in the air. Once she had pointed, laughing, at his nether regions but he had looked dreadfully affronted and hurt. He had clamped his leg down and that was the last she'd seen of his privates, which he'd taken off parade for ever. Now whenever he groomed himself he made sure she wasn't looking. But most unpleasant was his claw-cleaning routine – also usually done in the dark and involving a grating sound as he ran his teeth up and down inside his nails to scrape out the dirt.

There was no escaping his tail, either, which dominated her life. If she talked to him too much, particularly when he wanted to go to sleep, he would whack her with it. Thwack, he'd go across her hand, or even her face if he was feeling particularly evil. Thwack, thwack, thwack. Just you, thwack, shut, thwack, up, thwack. She usually did, although it was tempting to wind him up and start singing to him. 'How much is that pussy in the window? The one with the waggly tail,' she'd trill tunelessly. It worked every time, sending his tail into an exuberant frenzy, weaving like a cobra dancing to the sound of a pipe.

Gus's tail seemed like a separate entity that had been transplanted onto his body one day when his back was turned. The tail was annoyed by different things from the rest of him and controlled only by itself. Sometimes he looked at it as if it was an alien being and would capture it between his paws and sit on it, tucking it under him where it couldn't twitch any more. And on the stairs it was a nightmare. Maisie's stairs were narrow and steep and Gus had taken to sitting on look-out duty across the stairs with his tail out, weaving away as she tried to descend. Trying to dodge it was almost impossible. 'You'll be the death of me,' she said to him every morning as she tried to pass without falling headlong.

His tail wasn't only used as an annoyance, though. He also used it as a tool for greeting her when she'd been out, kinking it slightly and waggling it high in the air with a shuddery shake of a movement. It was most peculiar. Maybe, she thought, it was a left-over from his days as a tom and was full of strange-smelling emissions which he presumably wanted to squirt all over the place. Or maybe he really was part dog. That wouldn't have been surprising as her little niece Alex – the only one in the family with brown eyes – had gone through a stage of believing she was half canine. 'Look at Grandma's dog's big brown eyes and then look at mine, Auntie Maisie,' she'd said, aged seven. 'They're both the same, so we must be related.' It would have pleased Maisie's dad, who she was convinced would have preferred her to have given birth to a litter of puppies rather than had a baby. He was dead now – a merciful release after years of suffering progressively worse strokes – but he'd favoured animals over people any day.

Gus, though, hated dogs with a passion, as Maisie discovered when her middle sister Mandy came over with Katie, a soppy black Labrador puppy who was always pleased to see you, even if she'd only just left you a minute earlier. Gus had clearly been chased by a dog when he was younger, she thought, because he didn't hang around once a dog-owner entered the house. Within days of moving in with her, Gus had learned the voices of all her friends who had dogs and would zoom out through the catflap the minute he heard them.

His behaviour upset Maisie because it jeopardised her plans for Myrtle the basset hound. Maybe, she thought, Gus would be like Sky, Alex's cat, who'd started off hating the endearing black ball of puppy fluff that was Katie the Labrador and had then watched and waited until he had the measure of her. Sky learned how to control everything Katie did by positioning himself in key places around the home. If Katie was in the garden and it was dinner time, Sky would sit silently in the door of the kitchen, blocking her path. If the family were in the living room, Sky would sit in the hall, refusing to let Katie pass. His small but silent presence was so intimidating to the dopey dog it worked every time.

Would that happen with Gus? Maisie was now falling so completely under his spell that she couldn't bear to run the risk of him leaving her. Reluctantly, she decided to put her plan to get a dog on hold. 'It's only a temporary measure,' she warned Gus. 'One paw out of line and I'll reconsider.'

It was a logical move, though. A cat suited her far better than a dog because her work took her away almost every week and it suited Gus to be the only animal in her life. As summer drifted into autumn, Maisie started to wonder if he was taking over as the man of the house. Her friend Lucy who sometimes fed Gus when Maisie was away on business, said he was the sexiest beast in the village and she'd like a man just like him. That, though, didn't really say much because the single men in Cuckstone were, so far, downright disappointing.

'Move to the country, Maisie, out of gay Brighton, you're bound to find some nice farmer,' her townie mates had told her. Until now, though, the single men she'd met either weren't interested, were into hunting, which Maisie opposed with a passion, or were downright weird. But her friend John the gardener was coming over to give her a hand with the composting on Saturday and she'd always rather liked him. Maybe he would come up trumps...

On Saturday, Maisie put on her prettiest cotton dress, a faded and slightly ragged blue affair printed with washed-out pink roses. She straightened her wild hair, carefully applied her make-up to look as if she wasn't wearing any and put on a pair of flat, strappy silver sandals.

Knowing that John liked his food, she'd bought in some locally-cured bacon and fresh bread to impress him with her bacon butties. As he munched, she showed him round the house. Gus was nowhere to be seen.

'This is the back bedroom,' she said, artfully. 'It's a shame that next door's extension gets in the way of the view, otherwise you could see for miles over the fields. There's tons of wildlife out there and the dawn chorus every morning is so loud that it wakes me up. It's such a wonderful place to sleep and such an incredibly comfy bed.' She patted the bedspread in what she hoped was an enticing way. She was rather out of practice at flirting.

John, meanwhile, was oblivious to her wiles – or ignoring them – and was looking down into the garden. 'Is that your cat there?' he asked, pointing to a high brick pillar next to the back gate.

'I expect so,' Maisie replied, craning her neck.

'Wow!' exclaimed John. 'Did you see that?' All Maisie could see was that Gus had suddenly arrived in front of the bedroom window and was strutting proudly.

'He leaped from that pillar right up onto this flat roof. It must be about eight feet at least, and upwards rather than downwards,' said John. Maisie looked at Gus. He might as well have had his hands on his hips and be saying, 'Beat that, big guy. I'm the man about the house now.'

'I think he's seeing me off his patch,' said John, sagely. 'I'm glad I'm not your boy-friend, I wouldn't like to take him on. I've never had much time for cats, they crap on the garden and dig up your seedlings. Well, better start manuring.'

Maisie followed John downstairs, cursing silently, and let him get on with his work. Gus, meanwhile, strolled in and tucked into the biscuits in his dish. He looked rather pleased with himself, she thought.

'You've blown it for me, you rotten cat, and I've been hoping for months that John and I would get it together,' she whispered. 'Is this your plan, then? Are you going to sabotage all my relationships?'

PAWNOTE: When she said that I just

looked at her as if butter wouldn't melt in my mouth. I believe it's what humans call a blank stare – at least I hope it was because I don't want to show my hand. I used the look that I've adopted when I'm accused of something I didn't do, or want to pretend I didn't do, which amounts to the same thing as long as I don't get found out. It's the same look I use when I'm disappointed in my food. I sit there on my haunches, front paws neatly together, and stare at the dish she's just put down and which has so disappointed me. Then I glance up at her, meeting her eyes, and pointedly glance back down at my dish, then up again. In the end she always gets my meaning, although it took quite a while to get her to understand what I'm saying. Usually I get another dish of cat food out of it, which with luck will be to my liking second time around.

In this case, though, I just wanted to divert her attention from the display I'd put on for that man. No, I didn't want him round the house. He smelled very strongly, for one thing, and although that's probably because of his job it would literally get up my delicate nose. But the main reason was that I don't like gardeners. I was chased around the allotments by one who was tending his little patch of vegetables. The ground there is nice and soft, so it's a good place for a cat to go when he wants to do his business in peace. I am a very tidy animal and clear up after myself, burying any evidence deep down, but on this occasion I had just finished scraping up some very fine earth that had been piled into neat little heaps and was ideal for my purpose when he roared over brandishing a spade. It took me by surprise and I was forced to run for my life, so it's no wonder I'm wary of them.

I was over the allotments the other night, on the lookout for a nice mouse to bring my mistress. It took a long, long time to find a suitable gift for her and I spent hours crouched in the balmy darkness, listening to the cries of owls out hunting and waiting for a young mouse to come my way. I kept deathly quiet when I spotted a slinking dog fox – you never know how they're going to react and even cats in the prime of life, like me, could be in danger if we crossed a hungry fox. Then, soon after the fox had passed my hidey-hole, I heard that tell-tale rustle in the undergrowth. It's not a sound any human would be able to pick out but my ears are attuned. The scuffling came nearer and as it passed me I pounced out of my hiding place and collared it. It was a baby field mouse and I played with it for a bit, tossing it around, then letting it run away before putting my paw on its tail (I swear they stretch like boiled spaghetti when I do that). In the end it wasn't running away fast enough so I got bored and because I didn't want to spoil my present, I picked it up in my jaws and took it home.

Well, you wouldn't believe the reception I got after all my hard work. She was so ungrateful I wondered why I'd bothered. Admittedly it was 3am but time passes when you're on a stake-out. In the past I'd heard her saying she didn't mind mice although she'd have a problem with rats but she made such a fuss. The problem began as I manoeuvred the mouse through the catflap and he started to wriggle again. This reminded me that there was a bit of fun to be had before I delivered my gift, so I started a mouse chase around the dining room and up the wooden stairs. When I caught it again I brought it upstairs, still alive, and dumped it on her bed.

My mistress shrieked, jumped out of bed and tried to catch it but the mouse ran up the curtains and sat trembling on the wooden curtain pole. 'Gussie!' she yelled. 'You bad cat, don't you know what time it is?' I treated that fatuous question with contempt and totally ignored her but I did think it was time to make myself scarce and I decided it might be wise to sleep downstairs.

In the morning, of course, she forgot about the mouse and pulled the curtains and it fell off the curtain rail where it was still sitting in terror, landing on her shoulder and then zooming under the bed. I heard the commotion and knew it promised more entertainment, so I ran upstairs ready to chase it. I was only doing my duty as I cornered it in her office but she kept yelling, 'Get off the mouse, you horrible cat.' If I was sensitive I'd be offended but she's to be pitied really because she simply doesn't understand how we cats function.

Finally she cupped her hands gently round the mouse and took it downstairs to release it into the garden. 'Freedom and safety for you at last, my little one,' I heard her whisper, sentimentally. 'You live to squeak another day.'

But I had other plans for that mouse. It wasn't going to escape me so easily after all the work I'd put in and later that afternoon she found its dead body on the lawn, puncture wounds in its neck. Let that be a warning to her: there is no escaping the wrath of the cat.

By night time it seemed I was forgiven (and so I should have been, I was only doing what comes naturally). She's convinced herself I want a cuddle every night and that's why I'm pestering her to go to bed. But what I want is to see her tucked up tight. That way I know she's not in any trouble, not catting around the village or squashed like a hedgehog in the road. So about 10.30pm, which is late enough for any cat, I start to pace about. When she goes upstairs I jump on the bed, parade around while she speaks to me, then settle down in my favourite spot just below the pillow. It's soft there and away from draughts. Only when she turns the light off - and that can take hours if she's fiddling about with one of those rustly things that suddenly snap shut, which she calls a book – can I take myself off to bed and relax, knowing she's safe. Over time I've learned it's safer to sleep in my basket. There are less nocturnal interruptions and I don't get kicked off the bed when she turns over.

People say cats don't have a sense of humour and we like to preserve this myth as it serves us well. But it isn't true. I find the 'phoofff' sound she makes when I land on her bed with four heavy, concrete paws in the middle of the night is well worth the disruption to my sleep. A variation is to jump up with my feather paws on so she doesn't know I'm there and wait until she snores. Then I put my concrete paws on and land – hard – on top of her. I get a good noise from that one, too, but I usually get booted off the bed, so the result isn't great. Once she even threw a slipper at me, so I will keep this one for when she's been away on holiday and I'm really annoyed with her.

There's a good trick I play in the garden, too. I wait until she's dozing in the sun on her sunlounger, then I walk quietly up to her and run my tail across her throat. 'Uuurrgghh,' she goes. Oh, if a cat could laugh... But don't laugh at *me*. Cats aren't meant to be funny. She did that once, laughed, out loud, at my private part which is all I have. Its companions were cut off in their prime but it doesn't stop me being less of a cat. I am all male, whatever those butchers did to me when I was a kitten. And I am determined not to allow another male in my house.

Chapter Four

Intruders in the House

Gus did not have many enemies in the village – in fact there weren't many cats at all living nearby but then they'd probably been wiped out by the evil road that cut Cuckstone in two. Before she moved in, Maisie had been unaware that what was a narrow B road became a rat run in the morning and evening rush hour (all two-and-a-half hours of it) and at weekends. In her first summer in the village she'd witnessed a beefy red-faced woman take off her jacket and, in a fit of swearing that turned the air blue (and which an elderly neighbour had described quaintly as 'very salty language'), threatened to punch the effing daylights out of a doctor who'd politely asked Mrs Beefy to reverse as he was on his way to see a sick patient.

'I'm going to f...ing smack you,' Maisie heard Mrs Beefy yell, as she went back to the car, removed her tight jacket with its attractive crescents of sweat under the armpits and proceeded to bear down on the slight young doc, meaty fists swinging. In the end Mrs Beefy had chickened out before landing the first punch in front of all those witnesses yelling at her to reverse her bloody car or else and had roared off in a flurry of filthy words, taking his wing mirror with her.

Similar, although not such entertaining, incidents occurred almost every week, usually involving Maisie and her neighbours losing bits of their cars or having them bashed or scratched. It had cost her a fortune in voluntary excess payments since she'd moved to Cuckstone. Meanwhile, friends down the road were heartbroken after losing their two adorable adolescent kittens to drivers who roared through the traffic-calming measures at night swiping anything and everything in their path. The kittens hadn't stood a chance as they stood on the edge of their driveway sniffing the air.

Maisie had recently become friends with a neighbour called Sasha Penrith, who lived opposite with her dogs and cat in an ancient half-timbered cottage that once housed the local blacksmiths. Sasha's cat, a sinuous, yellow-eyed beast called Scabby, was Gus's arch enemy and they were always scrapping. During the latest spat, Scabby's collar had come off and she'd found it lying on her doorstep, so one wet October evening Maisie decided to pop it back to Sasha and catch up with the gossip.

Sasha's doorpull on the forge was a long, dangling affair with an iron handle. Maisie gave it a hefty tug and heard the bell tinkling inside and the barking of two dogs: the deep woof woof woof of Pluto, the handsome broad-headed Labrador, and the high-pitched yap of the world's naughtiest Jack Russell, aptly named Tinkerbelle. In the short time Maisie had known Tinkerbelle she'd taken an overdose of Pluto's arthritis pills and had had to have her stomach pumped, and had eaten her way through most of a seven-pound bag of dog meal and had lain on the cold kitchen floor groaning. If ever a dog needed long enough paws to rub her tummy with, Tinkerbelle did then, but her stumpy legs were too short to get anywhere near her distended belly.

Originally two cottages dating back to the 14th century, Sasha's house had been knocked into one to form a long, low building which, unlike most cottages, was flooded with light during the day. It was a place

Sasha adored but now she was distraught. She had confided in Maisie over a few large gin and tonics that her philandering husband, who Maisie had never met, had gone off with another woman and she was having to sell her beloved cottage, dismantle the family home and all the possessions she'd accumulated over the years and move to heaven knows where, away from all her friends.

'I don't know what to do or where to go,' she'd said. 'We've been together for almost 20 years and although we weren't what I'd call happy, we had our moments. Now I hate him for doing this to me and to our son and I'm about to lose everything we worked so hard for because he's making me sell the house and split the proceeds. And she's much younger than me and she's bound to want to have a family with him and I couldn't bear that.'

Maisie had tried to tell Sasha that being single and independent wasn't necessarily a bad thing but she could see that if you'd been with somebody for years then the thought of having to start again, on your own, in your mid-50s, wasn't an enticing or exciting prospect. It certainly explained why so many people, fearing a lonely old age, stuck it out in marriages where love had left years before. But Sasha was slim, witty and raven-haired and she wasn't going to be on the shelf for long, Maisie was sure.

Maisie pulled on the bell again, just as the front door was opened by a short but attractive, dark-haired man, which threw Maisie and she started burbling. 'Oh sorry,' she said, 'I was looking for Sasha. I have her collar to return. Well, not *her* collar as such, Sasha doesn't need a collar, well not often, only when she's had too much wine, it doesn't agree with her like G & T does and it goes to her knees. A collar would be great then because we could put her on a lead and...'

Maisie fell silent as the man extended a well-manicured and surprisingly soft hand. 'Marcus Nesbit, Sasha's solicitor,' he introduced himself. 'And you are?'

'Hi, I'm Maisie Maddox, I live opposite. You see that little house over there, diagonally opposite, well that's mine, it's a bit small but I really like it.' SHUT UP you idiot, Maisie thought to herself. Don't prattle. You must fancy him, that's why you're behaving like a halfwit.

'Very nice,' said Marcus, glancing down the road. 'Do you want to speak to Sasha?'

At that point her friend came to the door, much to Maisie's relief.

'Hello dear, want a G & T?' she said. 'I see you've met Marcus, he's staying for one – we've just finished discussing the divorce and we both need a stiffener after that.'

Maisie accepted gratefully and sank down onto the sofa. One of Sasha's gins was pretty hefty but after five on an empty stomach she was reeling – and burbling on to Marcus about anything and everything. He was a lovely man, she decided, as she rose unsteadily to go to the loo – very urbane and charming and he seemed to be interested in her life, which was unusual. He'd asked all about her travels abroad, her job and her past boyfriends and she, of course, had told him in great detail. Poor Sasha couldn't get a word in edgeways.

'Well, musht go,' she slurred, wobbling back into the room. 'Thanksh sho much, Shasha. My turn nexshtime.'

'I'll walk you home,' said Marcus. Gallant and such a gentleman, thought Maisie, hazily. Why don't I meet men like this more often?

Marcus took her arm and guided her across the road and up her front path. He'd only been drinking Evian water because he was driving, so he was quite steady on his feet as she stumbled along beside him.

'Fancy meeting up again, Maisie?' said Marcus, pecking her on the cheek as she tried to get her key into the lock. 'Here, let me do that for you.' The door swung open to reveal the chaos inside – Maisie hadn't tidied up for a while and newspapers and books were everywhere.

'Would love to, Marcush, you're a gent!' said Maisie, swiftly pulling the door to behind her. 'When do you want to meet?' She knew as she said it that she sounded a bit desperate and should be playing it cool.

'I'll ring you,' he said. 'Give me your number and I'll put it into my phone.' Maisie did as she was told for once.

'Look forward to hearing from you,' she shouted after his retreating back. 'We'll have lotsh of fun!'

Gus gave Maisie a dirty look as she came in. He usually waited for her to come in before he went out himself – to prove a point, she'd always thought. It was like being married to a grumpy old man.

She poured herself a glass of wine – might as well make my hangover worthwhile because I'm going to have one anyway, she reasoned – picked up the phone and dialled her friend Jenny in Devon. 'Guessh what, I think I've met a nishe man,' she said. 'Whatsh more, he's ashked me out. Whadya think of that?'

The next morning Maisie woke up on the sofa, her head pounding, her mouth tasting like a badger's armpit would probably taste if only she'd tried it. 'Oh God,' she groaned, remembering how she'd talked at Marcus for hours and given away all her secrets. It was one of the main problems with working from home and living alone. You became so deprived of human company that when you did see people you either couldn't string two sensible words together because you were out of practice or you went the other way and got totally over-excited and yabbered for England. I was so over-eager I've probably blown it, she thought. I don't expect I'll hear from him again.

Later in the day, though, Sasha rang to say that Marcus had been singing her praises and was looking forward to their date. 'Surprising,' said Maisie, 'given I talked absolute rot all night. But I'll wait and see if he rings.'

And wait she did ... for two weeks and until she'd given up all hope of hearing from him. If they are serious about wanting to take you out they usually ring within a couple of days, thought Maisie. He was clearly just another flasher in the pan and she'd had plenty of those over the years.

But one evening, after coming back exhausted from a long walk, the phone rang as she walked in. 'Yup?' she barked, as she fell over the rug, 'Maisie here.'

'It's Marcus,' said a smooth voice at the other end. 'We met at Sasha Penrith's the other day. I said I'd call you.' Yes, you did you slimy bastard, thought Maisie, but her voice was already responding with an entirely different message.

'Oh, how lovely to hear from you,' she heard herself gushing. 'How are you? I do hope you're well. Are we going to meet up?'

She could have bitten her tongue off at that point. Talk about being too eager. There was a pause at the other end, then Marcus replied. 'You are keen, aren't you? How sweet. I'm ringing to ask if you'd be free for a drink tonight.'

Maisie knew she should say no. He wasn't giving her any notice, which meant he'd probably been let down by somebody else but what the hell. Handsome men with a bit of money – he was a solicitor after all – didn't come her way very often these days and what had she got to lose?

'Love to,' she replied. 'Just give me time to get ready and then we can meet. Where do you suggest?'

They agreed to get together in an hour at her local, The Bell. It was a gastropub these days and although the chef could be a little unpredictable with his portion sizes and seasonings, there was usually a good choice of locally-produced food on the menu and it seemed easier than trying to find some-where else. Anyway, if she didn't have to take the car, she could get rid of her nerves with a few glasses of vino.

Maisie raced upstairs and into the shower. 'I've got a date, Gussie,' she told the cat. 'How about that? I might even bring him back. Now if I do, you have to be nice. No showing off, no macho behaviour, just go to bed in your basket and behave.' Gus yawned lazily and curled up in his bed. It was covered in red roses and rather sissy for a male cat but he was masculine enough to cope. If he'd been a man, she thought, he'd have been the sort to wear a pink shirt with pride and there'd have been nothing gay about him.

She went through her wardrobe. As usual there was nothing that seemed quite right for the occasion. Jeans? Too casual and they didn't do her rather large bottom any favours anyway. Smart trousers? Too manly and work-like. A sexy black dress? She'd probably given him the wrong impression already, she didn't want to appear too easy. He was quite smarmy, she decided, but it was nothing a few glasses of wine wouldn't fix. She sighed. A viable boyfriend hadn't been on the cards for ages and the smell of neglected woman was hanging round her like the stench of a dead albatross.

This was a phrase she and her Devon friends had cooked up many years ago: the albatross. You officially got the albatross if you hadn't had sex for more than a year and it gave you that smell of desperation that Maisie had named 'soul odour'. The only thing to do was to get rid of it as soon as you could, then you were albatross-free for another year and the smell of a desperate woman in need of some male attention had retreated. Recently Maisie had accumulated a number of albatrosses (or was it albatrossi?). They were hanging off her now in invisible rows and it was high time she did something about it.

With minutes to go she decided on a flared skirt that hid her bulges and teamed it with brown suede boots and a lowish-cut T-shirt that showed off the best bit of her physique – her cleavage. Maybe my luck's changing at last, she thought, as she pranced down the street feeling at one with the world. Although she was 10 minutes late – he won't mind, she thought, it's a woman's prerogative and anyway I spent it making myself look gorgeous for him – Marcus was nowhere to be seen. Maisie bought herself a large glass of Merlot and perched on a bar stool to talk to Viny, the landlord.

'Looking a bit glam tonight, Maisie, what're you up to?' inquired Viny, who was more used to seeing her in muddy jeans and wellies.

'Got a date, Viny,' said Maisie. 'Oh look, here he is now.'

Marcus sauntered over, dapper in a pair of taupe chinos and a blue linen shirt that matched his eyes. She'd thought they were brown but now she could see they were the colour of dark blue sapphires – and hard like sapphire chips, too, she thought. He does know how to dress to make the most of himself, he's a bit of a peacock.

He kissed her rather too intimately on the mouth, which she wasn't sure she liked. There was something a bit possessive about it, as if he was laying claim to her in front of Viny.

'I see you've got a drink so I'll just get one for myself,' he said. 'Now, do they have a menu with something worth eating on it?' Maisie could see Viny frowning and willed him to keep quiet. He wasn't known for his tact if someone insulted his pub and particularly its food but for once he didn't come up with a pithy put-down.

Saying he was watching his weight and patting his rounded stomach to prove it, Marcus ordered himself a salad. Maisie had set her heart on a hefty rack of lamb with her favourite Dauphinoise potatoes but not wanting to seem greedy she changed her order to grilled sea bass on a bed of spinach.

'OK to go halves, Maisie?' Marcus said. 'I know you independent career girls, you don't like to feel beholden to us men.'

What can I say? thought Maisie, who hadn't been paid for some weeks. 'Yes, fine by me, you know us women these days,' she replied. God, was he mean as well as conceited? The evening was almost over before it had started. But as they took their seats in the corner of the old coaching inn and the wine unthawed Maisie's tongue, she found she was enjoying herself. Marcus was interesting company and he insisted on buying her glass after glass as she chattered away, telling him how she'd moved to the village not knowing anyone and how she'd been adopted by Gus. To give Marcus his due, he appeared to listen and he talked quite a bit, too. She found out he was single, and like her had never been married although he wasn't sure about having children. He spent his holidays exploring far-flung bits of the globe and was keen on scuba-diving, something she'd never tried. He didn't like animals, though, which was a big minus point.

By the time Viny called last orders, Maisie was full of bonhomie and good wine. 'Back to my place for coffee then, Marcus?' she asked, grasping his arm.

'Love to, Maisie,' he said, winking at her.

They lurched up the high street together and as they reached Maisie's front door, Marcus took the keys from her and let them in, pulling her behind him. Pushing her up against the living room door, he kissed her. 'Been dying to do that all night,' he said, groping under her T-shirt. 'You're really hot...'

Maisie was feeling slightly overwhelmed as they snogged their way up to the bedroom and onto her vintage French bed. She didn't usually sleep with a man on the first date and this was getting out of control. First date sex was more often than not a disaster – either the sex was no good, in which case you wanted to try again to make it better, or it was great and you wanted more but because you'd given your all too early they had no respect for you and never rang again. Either way it was lose-lose but this time she seemed to have lost control. Just go with the flow, she told herself, you know you need to dump the albatrossi.

At that point she glanced at the end of the bed. There was Gus, sitting bolt upright, his hair on end. He looked huge and his peridot eyes were fixed on Marcus with absolute hatred.

'Mmmmm Marcus,' said Maisie, wrenching her mouth from his.

'Mmmmm Maisie,' he replied, fastening his lips back on hers like a suction pump.

'No, Marcus, stop,' said Maisie, pulling away. 'I can't do this with Gussie on the end of the bed, I really can't. Somehow it's embarrassing, I don't want him to see. I have to get him off the bed, just hang on a mo.'

She went to move but Marcus held onto her. He was quite strong, she realised. He clapped his hands loudly at Gus and pointed to the door. 'Get off the bed NOW,' he ordered but Gus just sat there refusing to move and continued to glare furiously at Marcus. That's most unlike him, thought Maisie, he usually runs out at the first sight of a stranger. Maybe he thinks he's protecting me. Even I'm not sure that sleeping with Marcus is a good idea now.

'Hang on a mo,' said Marcus, moving down the bed. He put out his foot, still in its black silk sock and kicked – literally kicked – Gus off the bed.

'Bloody cat,' he said as Gus, with a loud miaow of pain and an even louder one of outrage, bolted for the door. 'There, that's got rid of him.'

Maisie was aghast. Too stunned for words – a rare reaction for her – Marcus took advantage of her silence to grab her and try to kiss her again. 'Now, where were we?' he murmured.

'Get OFF ME,' she shouted as she found her voice. 'How dare you kick my cat? How DARE you? You don't treat any animal like that, especially not if you want to impress me.'

Marcus looked at her nastily. 'Impress you? Get over yourself, Maisie, you know you're gagging for it,' he said. 'You're an easy lay, I can tell. You've been draping yourself all over me ever since we met at Sasha's. Don't be such a prick tease. Now we've got rid of that ruddy cat, let's get into bed. Come on, you know you want to.'

Maisie couldn't believe her ears. 'I thought after we'd spent the evening together that we had lots in common but you're only after one thing,' she said. 'I told you how much that cat meant to me and you shouldn't have kicked him. You might have hurt him. How can I go out with you knowing you treat animals like that?'

'Go out with me?' said Marcus, with a spiteful laugh. 'You must be joking. I don't go out with women of your age – or your size, for that matter. I like my women young and petite. No, this was a mercy shag. You looked as if you could do with one and you were certainly up for it. How long's it been?'

Maisie couldn't speak, she was so affronted. And angry. And ashamed of herself for being such a fool.

'Get out of my house,' she said at last, in a quiet but steely voice. 'I never want to see you again. You are a truly horrible little man.'

Marcus realised he'd gone too far. 'OK, OK, keep your hair on,' he said, pulling on his shoes and heading for the front door, which Maisie slammed and locked behind him. Once she knew he was out of earshot she burst into tears. Sobbing, she tried to find Gus who had long since disappeared into the night. She knew he'd be back, though. There was nothing faithless about that cat.

Marcus's words stung like mad but as Maisie calmed down she comforted herself with the fact that she'd had a lucky escape. How much worse would it have been to have slept with him and found out afterwards what he thought of her? At least she'd escaped with some fragment of pride intact.

Straightening the rumpled covers, she crawled into bed. Single life might be lonely at times but imagine if she was married to a total bastard like Marcus, she reasoned as she tried to sleep, her mind racing with the turn events had taken. If he was the last man on earth and it meant she'd never have sex again in her lifetime she wouldn't want him. At that point there was a little "ow?' from the side of her bed and Gus appeared to curl up beside her. No, give her the love of a good cat any day.

PAWNOTE: I am outraged and ashamed. My head is hanging low, for I have been beaten on all counts recently. I am losing my touch.

First I lost a fight to the evil Scabby Penrith. I hate that animal with a passion, with his evil, slinky ways and voracious appetite for other cats' food. Ever since I was a kitten he has tried to intimidate me. As a youngster I kept my distance and fostered my grievances but since I reached cathood I have always fought back. Sometimes I win, sometimes Scabby is the victor and over the years we've inflicted some vicious bites and scratches on each other. I hated him even more after he clawed me so badly with his filthy nails that the wound became infected and my previous owners took me to the vet. It makes me shudder to recall how I was made to sit in a room full of dogs – an absolute horror for a cat of my disposition who was once chased by a demented, baying hound – and then a stranger took me in a stranglehold, stuck something cold and thin up my bottom and washed out my wound with a solution that stung so badly I almost jumped out of my beautiful fur coat. It was agony – and it's given me a loathing of Scabby that will last our lifetimes.

When I was younger, I was so much sharper than I am today. I would sit silently and wait, all day if need be, for Scabby to saunter by. Then I would attack before he'd registered my presence. These days, though, I am more content. I admit, I have fallen in love with my mistress and it has meant I've lost some of my snappy, streetwise ways. I'm just not as keen on a scrap as I once was.

Like me, Scabby has no balls yet he's never ducked a fight and the other day was no exception. Many adjectives fit his description and all of them are sinister. He is a most menacing cat and casts malevolent amber glances at all two- and four-legged beasts, except his owner. I have found out he behaves like a lap cat at home and drapes himself around her neck like an old fur collar. It's something I like to taunt him with. He wasn't born and bred here – he was a Londoner who had rarely gone outdoors until he arrived in Cuckstone. Initially the country terrified him but as he became bolder, the lure of the fields and hedgerows, packed with mice and birds, beckoned him away from the hearth. From spending most of his life indoors, Scabby began to roam, spreading his territory – and his reign of terror – ever wider.

Although he lives over the road he seems impervious to the dangers posed by impatient and inconsiderate drivers and has developed a roving habit that takes him far and wide. He has been spotted on the side of various roads, testing the tarmac with his talon-clawed paws for vibrations and then sauntering across at his leisure. He is also an unwanted guest at every catflap in the village, including my own.

Scabby is getting on now and to make up for his lack of speed he has become slyer, which is why he caught me out the other day. I had just woken up from an 18-hour sleep and had wandered downstairs for breakfast but my mistress served me with a dish of sardine chunks, which I have made quite clear that I hate, so I miaowed to go out. Why should I use a cat flap when there's someone available to open the door for me?

But as I wandered out onto the terrace, sniffing at the ground to check for intruders, Scabby rounded the corner out of nowhere. He was on two legs and going at a gallop, using the element of surprise to pounce. I jumped two feet into the air and as Scabby leapt for my neck I bolted for the cat flap, thinking I could escape – but my stupid mistress had forgotten to unlock it from the inside.

I was wedged – my face and front half squashed up against the plastic door of the cat flap and my backside being duffed up from behind by Scabby. Then I had to be rescued! Oh, the disgrace. 'Get away from him, Scabby, you brute,' I heard her shout as she grabbed the pugnacious tabby by the collar, which came off in her hands. 'Go on, scat.'

He took one last vicious snap at my protruding bottom and fled down the garden path, leaving me to scuttle inside and lick my wounds, which amounted to a bit of pulled fur and a lot of injured pride.

But that was nothing compared to the other night when she brought back a man. One of my jobs here is to protect her from her own worst judgement and he was an odious piece of work. I did what I could – I sat on that bed and although I was nervous, because he was so much bigger than me, I refused to move. Then she, too, tried to get rid of me! Doesn't she understand that I am meant to look after her? I am, after all, the man of this house. But her companion presumed he was boss and first he shouted at me, then he kicked me! I jumped out of the way and he only caught me a glancing blow with his big toe but even so.

If I hadn't been afraid of getting badly hurt I would have laid into him with my teeth and claws but I could tell he was a man who didn't like animals and would stop at nothing. So I retreated and watched and waited. My mistress was in danger and I was frightened when she put on that terrible voice, all low and fierce and cold. It reminded me of the day she'd caught me peeing on her armchair. When she spoke to me like that I had to run outside in shame and I have never done it again. But that special voice of hers must work on humans, too, for the same thing happened with the man, only he hasn't come back.

After she'd locked him out she was crying. I waited for her to go to bed – I'm not very good with emotional scenes – and when she'd stopped sobbing I jumped up beside her and curled up as close as I could get next to her. 'Oh Gussie,' she said, 'why can't men be more like you?' They are my sentiments precisely and I am glad she spoke them out loud. I don't understand why she doesn't just leave things as they are. We are happy together, we're male and female. Why does she need to introduce a man to her world when she knows what problems it causes?

Chapter Five

The Reign of Saddam Hissein

Maisie was sitting on her terrace enjoying the late February sunshine. It was nippy but bright and after a disgustingly wet and grey winter, which had left the ground so sodden that walking was more like skating on mud, the pale, glittery sun was a welcome sight. She looked round her garden. The tulips she'd planted in the autumn were poking their wayward green shoots up through the dark earth in the plant pots and her favourite Pheasant's Eye narcissi were coming into bud.

It won't be long now until April and things start to come out, thought Maisie. And then it's May, best month of the year and the time when something good always happens to me. She looked over at her neighbour's entrancing garden planted with snowdrops in drifts of white.

There's Gus, she thought, looking up at her neighbour's shed. A rounded black cat was sitting on the felted roof, gazing round as he surveyed his territory. He doesn't usually sit there, it must be his new surveillance post. Goodness, he looks rather fat. I must put him on a diet.

A thought occurred to her. She'd just left Gus upstairs in his current favourite snoozing spot – on her beautiful Chinese satin and velvet bedspread in the back bedroom, which he'd sneaked onto when she wasn't looking. He'd been fast asleep only a few moments ago. Must have slipped past me, I suppose, thought Maisie, and forgot all about it.

But the next day, as she turned the key in the lock of her candy pink front door, she smelled a strange odour. It seemed to seep along the floor and waft out to meet her nostrils in insidious fashion, winding up them and lodging just below her sinuses. Tom cat, she thought, I recognise that smell. But Gus had been neutered years before. Surely he didn't have the necessary equipment to produce such a rank emission? She hadn't noticed him regrowing any dangly bits despite his macho behaviour towards John and Marcus.

Wandering into the kitchen, her nose on red alert, Maisie caught sight of an oily yellow spray mark on the skirting board. Could that be the evidence, she wondered? Was there another cat around? She sniffed. Yup, this was the malodorous culprit. Gus, meanwhile, was nowhere to be seen, which was unusual as most days he miaowed up to her and curled round her legs when she'd been out.

Calling him, Maisie went upstairs.

'Oh there you are, boy,' she cried, spotting him on the pristine white cotton duvet on her bed. But he didn't look quite right. There was no look of love in his eyes, just a blank stare. His coat was a dusty black, like a much-washed T-shirt, not glossy and gleaming like Gus's pelt, and he was hunched up rather than stretched out.

Behind her she heard a tiny "ow?'. There was Gus, emerging from the back bedroom, slinking low to the floor as if he was trying to make himself as unobtrusive as possible. Who, then, was on her bed? Or rather, what? Was this a clone? Was it a relation of Gus's? At that point the intruder jumped off the bed, hissed at her as he wandered arrogantly past as if he had all the time in the world, and stalked down the stairs. Gus was still hiding behind her legs.

'Not like you to be scared, boy, is it?' she

said, tickling him behind his ears. 'Who's that, your daddy? He looks just like you without the Burmesey bit. More to the point, what's he doing in our house?' Maisie went downstairs and wiped the skirting board clean, hoping that was the last she'd seen of Gus's doppelganger.

The following morning, though, she found more stinking emissions on the skirting board and Gus's food bowls were licked whistle-clean. He never finished all his food, habitually leaving enough for a couple of mouthfuls should times get hard – a habit, Maisie presumed, left over from when he was down on his luck and didn't know where his next meal was coming from. The rogue black cat had clearly been in the house and scoffed everything he could find, then marked the place as his – and his alone. No wonder poor Gus was scared. Although they looked more or less a match size-wise, the intruder was more solid than the long and sinuous Gussie.

He's an evil beast, thought Maisie. I shall call him Saddam - Saddam Hissein – and he'd better watch out if I get hold of him. He'll be off to the vet for immediate castration.

But nothing and nobody stopped Saddam

and he continued his irregular visits over the following weeks, permeating the house with his strong, feral squirts, leaving Maisie to ferret out the source with her nose to the floor. Gus, meanwhile, became nervy, staying up all night on the stairs, alert and on cat-watch, and refusing to eat his food. He was obviously disturbed by this intruder in his home and he'd become reluctant to go outside unless Maisie was by his side.

Sasha had also had problems with Saddam, whose brass neck knew no bounds. He had weaselled his way into her house, despite the presence of two dogs who would have loved to have got their paws on a black cat, and sprayed on her jeans. She was half-way round her daily walk, thinking there was a dreadful smell in the air that morning, when she realised she was the one who was stinking.

If there were two of them being targeted by Saddam there were bound to be others, reasoned Maisie, who decided to advertise to try and find the cat's owner in the village magazine, the quirky Cuckstone Talkabout. She'd been a fan ever since she'd read how a man called Simon had squashed his pet squirrel by stepping on it. She knew it wasn't funny – she felt sorry for the man and even sorrier for the poor squirrel – but everyone she knew had found his story hilarious and Si's squirrel had been the talk of the village for weeks.

Her advert read:

EATS, SPRAYS AND LEAVES

Are you the owner of a short-haired, black, unneutered tom cat with green eyes, a pointed face and a thick, wide tail who frequents the catflaps of Cuckstone? This cat appears to be a stray – he breaks into our houses, terrorises our cats, eats their food, sleeps on our beds and sprays before he leaves.

If anyone recognises his description, please could they leave their details on the number below and I will get back to them. If I don't hear from anyone I will attempt to have this cat rehomed by an animal charity
Maisie Maddox.

Unfortunately nobody came forward to own up, leaving Maisie no wiser and Saddam continuing to make her life a misery. I know, I'll ask the girls for their advice when they come to dinner on Friday, she thought. This group of friends came from all over Sussex and a while back she'd nicknamed them the Cat Pack because of their love for their feline friends. The Devon lot preferred canines, she pondered, but they hadn't liked it when she'd suggested they call themselves the Old Dogs. Bitch Massive hadn't gone down too well, either.

Having been an honorary Old Dog (in her own mind) for many years, Maisie was now proud to be accepted as the newest member of the Cat Pack. Lucy was, she supposed, the original member because she was the first one to get herself a cat. Maisie and Lucy had known each other since they were at primary school together and, while they had very different personalities, their bond was strong and deep because they had spent so many years bound up in each other's lives and families.

Lucy, who with her toffee-coloured curls and English rose complexion had the looks of a milkmaid fresh from the dairy, had grown up on a farm surrounded by horses and donkeys, which Maisie spent the school holidays riding over the Sussex Downs. She'd got married young to a man who had bullied her mercilessly but her second husband was the flip side of her coin. Theirs was truly a symbiotic relationship and they were the strongest and happiest couple Maisie knew. One day she'd like a marriage as honest as theirs, although she doubted if she could ever sustain anything that interdependent. But although Lucy's marriage was wonderful, Lucy's cat George had been a great disappointment to her. A snooty ginger beast with unpredictable claws, he preferred the next door neighbour and adoption papers had now been served, to the satisfaction of all parties, Lucy had reported.

The second member was tall, skinny Viv, who Maisie had met when she'd written an article about Viv's lovely cottage in the nearby village of Lindfield. She owned three tabbies, who were her babies. These were the children she had wanted so desperately and never had, losing first her husband and then later in life, her lover, after she miscarried on both the occasions she'd got pregnant. In the past, Maisie had inwardly scoffed at cats being substitute kids but now she was happy to eat humble pie. Viv was right: cats could be the best companions and a single life with cats wasn't necessarily a worse life than one with a man and children, it was just different. It was certainly

better than being in an unhappy relationship with no easy way out, like Di, the third
Cat Pack member and an old secondary
school friend of Maisie's who lived in
London and was down for the night.

Her husband was an arse of the first order
and she had three bratty, spoiled kids to
look after single-handed, their behaviour a
result of overcompensating for the lack of a
father figure in their lives. Di's husband
thought it was enough to earn lots of money
in the City and pay the mortgage for their
over-embellished mock-Tudor house. That,
in his eyes, gave him the right to refuse to
participate in anything around the house.
He didn't run the kids to school, turn up at
open days, take them on treats or help Di
cook the meals. As for helping with the
washing up, that was a joke. Even at friends'
houses he sat there while everyone else ran
around clearing up after him. Maisie usually
gave him a wide berth because after a
couple of glasses she was bound to have a
row with him. Why Di didn't divorce him
she'd never understand because the marriage really had run its course, taking with it
all Di's old bouncy confidence and turning
her into a woman who looked much older
than she was. Di never bothered these days

with dyeing her blonde hair, which was streaked with grey, and she usually dressed in jeans with an elasticated waist ('because they're comfy') and baggy tops which hung loosely and unflatteringly from her widest point.

Maisie supposed the marriage was like a pair of comfy old slippers to Di – she and her husband rubbed along OK doing their own thing, so there was no need to upset the applecart by splitting up and ruining their children's lives. It was a bit like Sasha's had been – unhappy, but not quite bad enough to take that huge leap into an unknown future on your own. But every so often Di and her husband had dreadful rows where he would hurl plates across the room because he was too emotionally constipated to express his frustration in words. Di certainly paid a price for her privileged existence, and Maisie knew it was one she would never be prepared to pay.

The only good thing Di's prat of a husband had ever done as far as Maisie was concerned was to buy Di a Siamese cat – one of the original, round-faced sorts, not the horrible pointy-faced, big-eared, inter-bred Siamese that were currently so popular. Di's Siamese – called Patpong after the saucy nightlife area of Bangkok but known as Pong for short – had proved to be a faithful friend, full of mischief and adored by her children.

Maisie and her friends had far more to discuss than just their cats' habits and quirky ways, though. A night when they were all free to have dinner together came along only about once a year, so there was always loads to catch up on. Luckily none of the Cat Pack were faddy eaters, so Maisie was free to make her favourite lamb and orange tagine with jewelled couscous. It was a fiddly dish to get together but then it cooked happily in the oven for hours, leaving her free to drink and chat with her friends until its warm, spicy aroma filled the house, declaring that it was time to eat.

As the four women tucked in to Maisie's hearty dinner around the white-painted dining table, Di said, 'So, men, Maisie. Any luck?' Maisie related the tale of John the gardener being seen off by Gus, and how he'd tried to protect her from the oleaginous Marcus.

'I think you should try Internet dating,' said Viv. 'I'm doing it – and I've just met someone quite promising, though it's early days yet. We've had four dates and he seems as keen as me, which is a rare thing. I'd recommend it any day.'

Although she was delighted for her friend, Maisie's heart sank. She had tried Internet dating before – and dating agencies and putting personal ads in the newspapers – and she found them all totally soul-destroying.

When she'd first moved to Brighton she had belonged to an expensive dating agency but resigned after they sent her a gay guy who clearly only wanted a trophy wife to compete with his brother. Then she'd tried the personal ads. Her all-time favourite letter (it was in the days before email) had been from an inmate of the Illinois State Penitentiary. It was a very long letter, which had instantly made Maisie suspicious because who on earth had the time to write long letters? Only those with time on their hands, that's who, and they were usually criminal, insane and wrote in green ink, or very, very old. Sure enough, this guy had written about how he'd been wrongly imprisoned for supplying crack cocaine – of which he was innocent, yer Honour – and was facing a 30-year stretch. Her second favourite letter had come from Lagos, suggesting she might like to pay for this chap to come over and could he bring some cash with him to pay her back? It was obviously a money-laundering scam, and she hadn't replied to either. The guy she'd liked best – a teacher of the deaf who she'd been on one date with – had never rung her again and when she'd contacted him a year or so later (nobody could accuse her of showing her hand too soon in those days) he'd been about to get married.

Internet dating had been worse than disastrous. There had been a succession of sick and injured applying for the post of potential boyfriend but although Maisie had a soft and compassionate heart, she didn't want to be a nurse. The short, squat man with the gammy legs who could barely walk had been quite witty but he really was wide and so very ... single. Maisie knew she was single but she hoped she didn't behave like a bachelor. They could be very set in their ways and many of them seemed to want a mother rather than a lover and girlfriend. The triple-heart-bypass patient was only 40 but smoked like a chimney and had got the hump when she got his name wrong and called him Kelvin (after the restaurant they were in) instead of Derek. The first was a definite improvement on the real thing, she'd thought. He should have been grateful.

Then there were the bitter divorcees who

she just knew hated women deep down but couldn't keep away from them, and the guys who thought if they bought you a Chinese meal they'd bought your body for the night and weren't interested in getting to know you slowly. Finally, there were the ones who just looked you up and down the second they met you as if you were a total disappointment. One man with the kind of jutting lower jaw Henry VIII would have been proud of had sat in the bar looking out to sea and refused to make eye contact with her for an entire hour while she chattered away trying to get him to respond. It had been a hideous experience.

As the years had rolled by, Maisie would join a new site, stick with it for three months, go off the boil as her self-esteem crumbled and then spend months licking her wounds before plucking up the courage to try all over again. She was about due another go and she knew Di was right. After all, she wouldn't meet anybody just sitting around working from home on her own. But oh, it was such a ghastly process.

By the time she'd thought through all this, the conversation had moved on slightly and the Cat Pack were discussing whether single women were a threat to married women. Di seemed a bit ambivalent on this one but Maisie wasn't surprised as her husband was probably shagging his secretary. He had never seemed the faithful sort and had even made a pass at her on one drunken occasion, implying she should be grateful for the attention as she wasn't getting it anywhere else.

'What gets me,' said Maisie, chipping in, 'is couples who never, ever ask you to dinner when you're single and the second you get a boyfriend say, "You must bring so-and-so over so we can get to know him better." You'd think they'd realise how insulting that is, that you actually merit being invited in your own right, but they just don't seem to get it, even though they've come to all your parties and dos over the years. You can't point it out without being downright rude so you never say anything and they never know how you feel.'

Viv nodded. 'I know what you mean, it happens all the time. Personally, I hate people who, when they finally get a boy-friend, drop their single friends, as if being in a couple is the only respectable and acceptable state to be.'

Di wasn't sure about that and felt she was being got at. Digging into a second helping of couscous, she said: 'But then all of you who are single want to meet a nice man. If you really were happy to be single and thought it was so socially acceptable, why are you still searching for a mate? You all say you're fine on your own but almost every-one wants to find somebody to share their lives with. I know it's what you want, Viv, and you, Maisie, too, so why not admit it? How often have you moaned about being alone on a bank holiday or on Boxing Day, when everyone else is with their families? Single life really isn't all that great, is it? Except, of course, you can stay in bed all weekend if you want to and that's some-thing we mums simply can't do.'

Maisie was choking on her tagine when Viv replied for her. 'Di, of course we want to meet someone but it's not that easy, you know, so we make the best of what we do have. If you don't, if you spend your life regretting what you don't have, it's a waste of a life, and let's face it, nobody has it all.

'We're just saying that if you're married with kids, however busy you are, you should still make the same effort with your single friends that they make with you, not leave them to do all the running. As for lying in bed all weekend, dream on. We have to do everything without any help, financial or otherwise. Nobody looks after us when we're sick and there's nobody to pay our bills if, like Maisie, you're freelance and have a bad month or somebody doesn't cough up what's owing. At least you married people have back-up – financially and physically. You might be married to an unhelpful tosser, Di, but he is there taking some of the burden off you and he does earn decent money.'

Maisie was in full agreement but she noticed Lucy, who was a peaceful soul, was keeping very quiet. Oh dear, this could all escalate into a huge row if they didn't rein it back.

At that point Gus walked in, stalking through the kitchen and up the stairs with a furious glare at them all.

'Let me give you a cuddle, little cat,' said Lucy, but Gus was having none of it. He didn't like Maisie having friends round to his house, even if they were female.

'Do you know, I've got a Gus lookalike,' said Maisie, taking advantage of the situation to change the subject. 'He's a feral tom that seems to rove the area and sprays disgusting yellow squirt all over the house. It is the vilest smell and it has really upset Gus.'

'I've seen that cat about,' said Lucy. 'He

won't have worried George but he's definitely been breaking into catflaps down our road. He seems to have a huge patch and wanders for miles. You need to keep him locked out, Maisie, he's nasty.'

But locking the catflap at night had already proved to be counter-productive. Hadn't Gus been beaten up from behind by Scabby because he'd been trapped when she'd locked it? Then again, Maisie had just read a book of cat psychology saying the catflap was the equivalent of her leaving her front door open all night to burglars. Anyone could break in at any time and some cats could be badly affected by marauding cats and adopt nervous habits, which was exactly how it was affecting Gus.

'I've named him Saddam Hissein, because he's a thoroughly bad lot and he hisses at me,' said Maisie, glad the conversation had entered smoother waters. 'I think he may be Gus's dad, he looks so like him round the head. Possibly because he's still got his balls, Gus won't fight him. He's the dominant cat when he comes in here and Gussie knows it.'

The rest of the evening was spent discussing cat characteristics, how to get rid of Saddam and the best Internet dating site for

Maisie to join. 'It'll be Plump Partners if I don't stop picking at this cheeseboard,' she joked. 'Gus and I both need to go on a diet, he's getting porky, too. We'll start tomorrow. Chocolate anyone?'

The next time Maisie saw Saddam, a few days later, he had an ugly great abscess under his right eye, oozing poison. She went out and spoke to him, putting her hand out gently towards his head. 'It's OK, old boy,' she said, 'I know I gave you a bad name but I don't really hate you, just the stink you make in my house and the way you upset Gus.' Gingerly she touched the top of his head and he let her stroke him gently for a second before backing off hissing, teeth bared. But she'd got close enough to see that the wound was almost down to the bone. It looked really nasty and in need of urgent treatment. How to help a cat, though, that was feral? She'd never get him in a cat basket, even if she had one.

She spent her morning – when she was supposed to be writing up an interview for a national newspaper with an actress who'd lost half her bodyweight – ringing around various cat charities to ask for help. Nobody, it seemed, gave a damn about feral cats. The best advice she got was to borrow a cat trap and bait it with chopped up pilchards, which she did but it was hopeless. Either the rain washed the pilchards away, the sun dried them up or Saddam was hoiking them out without getting caught. That cat was un-catchable, she thought.

Some weeks later she caught sight of him again on the garden steps. The abscess looked as if it had healed but his eyes seemed glazed and distant. Maisie was worried but she couldn't get near him. When he limped off he looked like an old cat, which would mean his legendary burgling skills were definitely diminished. He certainly hadn't been in her house to spray for a long time. She knew she could be asking for more trouble but she couldn't bear to see him starve, so, soppy as ever, she began to put food out at night which was always gone by morning.

The following Thursday, Maisie came in late from a meeting in London. She was due to go on holiday in a couple of days and was feeling de-mob happy and looking forward to a drink with friends that night once she'd packed her suitcase. Then, out of the corner of her eye she saw a movement near the catflap. It was Saddam, curled up in the corner. She moved slowly towards him but he barely registered her presence. There was no hissing, no growling, no backing away. He looked really ill. Reaching out her hand, she tentatively touched his back and was horrified to find it was just skin and bone. His thick black coat had been hiding the fact that he'd lost most of his bodyweight. That abscess must have poisoned his entire system, she thought.

'Poor old boy,' she murmured. 'You must need some food and drink.' She opened a tin of cat food, which he ignored – a first for Saddam – and poured him some milk, which he lapped at thirstily. She had an awful thought. Had he come into her kitchen to die?

She didn't want to try to pick him up – she knew better than to try to touch a wild cat that was probably in pain and could rip her arm to shreds or bite her with a pair of festering fangs. If she called out a vet they'd charge her, and she couldn't prove he was a stray who'd just wandered into her home to die. What if the vet thought she'd just called him in because she was tired of looking after a sick old cat?

Eventually Maisie decided to leave Saddam overnight and see how he was in the morning. If he died in the night, well it was probably the best thing and at least he wouldn't end his days in captivity. If he lived, maybe he'd be better in the morning and would have left of his own accord.

During the night, Maisie woke to the most frightful smell, like ammonia mixed with pear drops. She went downstairs and found Saddam had weed all over the floor, copious amounts that had run under the skirting boards and through the wooden floor. It must be his kidneys, she thought. I reckon they've packed up. He had crawled across the room to the other door and was feebly scrabbling at it, trying to get out. Gus, meanwhile, was standing watching. He showed no fear of Saddam now, which just went to show how ill the old cat was.

Maisie cleared up the mess, put a bowl of water and a soft blanket down near Saddam and went back to bed. Her mind was racing and she couldn't sleep. What should she do now? She decided that she'd ring the RSPCA first thing in the morning and get them to come out.

Maisie tossed and turned her way into a short snooze, then got up again at six to check on Saddam. He'd moved onto the blanket and looked peaceful until he opened his eyes, which were blurry with pain. Maisie knew he needed help immediately and rang the RSPCA's helpline number. A couple of hours later an inspector turned up, took one look at the sorry animal and went to get the cat catcher – a loop of wire on a long pole.

'He doesn't look good but I'm not taking any chances of him getting his claws into me,' she explained.

'That's why I couldn't catch him myself,' said Maisie. 'He is, as far as I've been able to establish, totally wild.' Saddam was hoiked unceremoniously by the loop and put into a cat basket where he lay, motionless, on the floor.

'I'll ring you later when I know the prognosis,' said the inspector, and with that she was gone. Maisie had barely had time to say goodbye to the old sod. She realised she'd become quite fond of him and that probably she was the only friend he had. It was a touching thought and it made her feel guilty for not doing more.

If only I'd managed to get him to a vet's before, she thought, maybe he'd have been in a better state. But if they'd tried to rehome Saddam it would have meant him spending weeks in a cage, which he'd have hated. He was wild and untamed and in his prime he'd been proud, potent, strong – and very scary. Somewhere in him, though, there was a soft spot. Maisie wondered if, like Gus, he'd also been trying to find the love of a good woman. If so, she'd really let him down but she couldn't have imagined having a cat like him in the house.

At that point the phone rang, interrupting her self-flagellation. It was the RSPCA inspector. 'Just thought you'd like to know the vet said there was no saving him, he was too ill and too far gone, so he's been put down,' she said. Maisie felt unreasonably sad. Saddam Hissein had been a chapter in her life she'd rather have done without when it began, but she now realised he'd brought something to her world that she was going to miss.

'Saddam's dead now Gussie, you have nothing and nobody to fear any more,' she said, stroking his black head. 'And if he was your daddy, I'm sorry. You must be feeling very sad.'

PAWNOTE: Sad? She has so much to learn. I do wish humans wouldn't anthropomorphise us four-legged creatures. Yes, Saddam was my father but I didn't like him and I felt nothing for him except fear and, although I don't like to admit it, respect.

Unlike Homo sapiens, we cats – or Felis catus to give us our official species name – don't love somebody simply because we're related to them. I obeyed Saddam and never got into fights with him but that's because he was bigger than me and he fought dirty. He scratched me once on my head and it went septic and that taught me not to tangle with tom cats that are intact in that department. It was a lesson I needed to learn as a cheeky young kitten, to respect my elders, and I have taken heed ever since.

Saddam – her name for him, not mine – was a thief and a scoundrel, a blackguard if ever there was one. He got my beautiful Burmese mother up the duff many years ago after she fell for his muscular, Mellors-type 'charm' and my sisters and I were the result. I was cursed in that I looked like him – my head was exactly the same shape and colour, although my eyes and my chocolate pelt resembled my mother's, and my body and slim, waving tail are pure Burmese. Only an idiot would mistake them for the stumpy, stunted tail and body of a moggy.

In his lifetime, Saddam fathered many litters in this village, which is why there are so many middle-aged black cats around now. He dined well at many houses, too, although he was not exactly an invited guest. Now he's gone and I can be King and supreme ruler of my own territory again. Why should I be anything but overjoyed?

Unlike those women I have to listen to regularly – the Cat Pack, as she calls them (and how wrong that name is for reasons I shall expand on in a second) – I like being on my own. I hear my mistress and her friends moaning about how they can't find a man but I don't understand why they can't be more like us felines. These women also complain when they have found a man, so it's not as if that is the answer.

Take that Di, for instance. She's always moaning about her awful husband. He's been making her unhappy for years, coming home late, spending too much time out on the tiles, shouting and swearing and throwing things, which cats hate. Humans forget that although cats are full of courage and cunning, we're also much smaller than a human and you have the capacity to do us great damage without much effort on your part. If I lived in a household that was filled with anger, I would leave and find myself another place to live. Patpong, I understand, makes herself scarce when he comes home. What kind of place is that for a woman to bring up a cat – in particular a sensitive Siamese?

Independence is good, not bad, and my mistress and her friends should take a leaf out of my book. She won't hear me miaowing with self-pity about not having a female to share my life with. We cats embrace our single lives, we give our affections only to those we choose and then only when we want to. It gives us the freedom to come and go as we please and that is worth everything to us. We live in the moment, which is what counts. The past has gone, the future may never happen, the present is all. We enjoy our lives for what we can get out of them right here, right now.

I will talk you through a typical day in the life of a cat, to illustrate how satisfying it can be to do your own thing and be beholden to nobody. I get up with the sun and eat immediately. My food bowl is waiting for me on the landing outside my mistress's bedroom (she is fully educated now). She sometimes objects to the smell of my cat food, particularly on hot nights, but she prefers that to being jumped on at dawn. Then I do my catly duty and miaow quietly at her bedside before jumping up – gently, I want her in a good mood - and cuddling up by her side.

Stroking reminds cats of being licked by their mother as kittens and it makes me feel secure but it's good for her, too, because it makes her relax. Most of us socialised cats – not feral beasts like Saddam – love to be stroked. But if we don't know you we will sniff your hand first and only then decide if you are allowed to touch us. This is because we like to be in control.

I have had to teach her how to stroke me in the way I like best – on the head, behind the ears and around the neck. Now I trust my mistress I will let her touch my tummy – in fact, when I'm feeling very secure I roll over and offer it to her, which is a sign of the utmost trust, although I doubt if she appreciates that. The more attention she has given me, the more affectionate I have become with her and the more rewarding both our lives are.

When I have had enough fuss in the mornings I get off the bed and go downstairs to suss out the day. I sniff at the catflap to check if anybody has been in and either sit at the back door or on the dining table scanning the garden for signs of animal life. When she comes downstairs I get her to give me breakfast – my dawn snack has long since been digested – and to let me out to check the garden wall and boundary fences and do general cat business. In summer I may stake out a mouse nest, then find a safe patch of sun in the garden to sleep in for the day but I must be careful not to burn my ears, where the fur is thin. Somewhere up high is best, where I am master of all I survey.

In winter I come back in and curl up on a bed. If I am cold I make myself a nest in the duvet cover and huddle beneath it. I have been told off when she has found me snuggled under the duvet like a human but surely she shouldn't deny me warmth on a chilly day?

At some point if she is at home I will miaow for more food. I don't need it but it is interesting to see what is forthcoming. Then I sleep all afternoon. The early evening is when I expect my major feed of the day followed by a long cuddle on the sofa. As I've said before, I don't do laps but I do like curling up next to a warm thigh.

If she goes out I have every right to be annoyed at her coming home late and I go out myself when she comes back. After all, somebody has to guard the house from intruders and if it isn't her it has to be me. If she has friends over I usually stay out for the evening and only come in to give them a good glare when I stalk up to bed. I often hear them say, 'Your cat wants us to go home,' and they're right but they never take the hint. Finally my mistress and I settle down for the night. I proffer her my velvet head for a few minutes, then I eat from my dish and go to bed in my rose-covered basket ... and the cycle begins again.

Can you see how liberating independence can be? You have to make the most of what you actually have rather than hanker over what you haven't got. Nobody has it all, so if you're single, enjoy your freedom. Don't wallow in regret, for that is the biggest waste of all.

Chapter Six

The Bottom-biter

Maisie finally bit the bullet and joined a dating agency. Well, she joined two but the first one, Guardian Soulmates, proved a total disaster. In one whole month she didn't have a single response to her ad, let alone to any of the emails she sent. In the end she was so annoyed that she changed the headline on her profile to read: 'Guys, you can all bog off' and then ticked them off roundly for not having the courtesy to answer her emails. Amazingly she got two replies to this. The first was from a very hairy Scotsman who sent her a poem of similar length to *The Lotos-Eaters*, ending every verse with the words, 'Are you there? Are you out there?' She didn't want to admit she was very much out there and, convinced his search hadn't ended yet, she broke her own golden rule and didn't answer.

The other from a decent-sounding guy in Dorset who called himself 'World's

Strongest Man' but when she suggested they correspond, his response was so weak she gave it up as a bad job. 'OK, if you want to,' he said lamely, in reply to her sparky email. 'I suppose it wouldn't hurt to give it a go.'

Licking her wounds again, she then joined match.com in the hope that if so-called quality with the Guardian's matchmaking service had proved so disheartening, the sheer quantity of men on match.com might mean one came up trumps. So far they hadn't exactly rolled in in spades but her hopes of meeting a diamond geezer were higher than the previous month's. She loved puns, did Maisie. Her dad, who had died just before she moved to Cuckstone, had taught her how to pun when she was a kid and there was no surer way to Maisie's heart than to challenge her to a punning match.

Tonight, though, Maisie had a date. She was determined she wouldn't drink too much this time and repeat her Marcus debacle, so she took the car to nearby Haywards Heath to meet Roger in a bar. They had not spoken by phone but had arranged through email that they were going to have a nice, civilised evening getting to know one another over a quiet meal and a glass of wine. She'd seen a picture of him and, while he looked a little cuddly, he wasn't unattractively fat. Anyway, she liked big men.

It was a beautiful summer's evening in June, balmy and soft, and Maisie had high hopes as she climbed into her Mazda. Unfortunately, though, Roger was a non-starter. He may be Roger by name but, Maisie decided in an instant, he would never be Roger by nature and certainly not Roger the todger. Just say you got to groping stage. Where on earth would you find it under that huge top half? It would be like playing hunt the thimble. He resembled one of those wobbly men who can't fall over, with short legs that looked too spindly for his gigantic frame, and a tiny Cupid's bow mouth pursed into a moue by excess jowl flesh. In the ad he'd said he was well-built but this was the man-sized equivalent of Ceausescu's palace in Bucharest. He was pleasant enough but it simply did not make up for his unattractive appearance.

Maisie was usually quite sympathetic to overweight people, being a tad on the big side herself, but when Roger ordered three starters – he said the portions were tiny in this restaurant – and demolished them in seconds, she began to wonder if he had an eating disorder. Wasn't there a strange condition where people couldn't stop eating? She knew she'd read about it somewhere. Oh yes, it was coming to her: Prader-Willi Syndrome. She'd cocked up again.

As the evening wore on – and on and on, as far as Maisie was concerned because nothing he could say was going to make her romantically interested in him – she plotted ways to escape. Excusing herself to go to the loo, she rang her friend Lucy. Thank God for mobiles. 'I need an excuse to get away,' she said. 'Ring me back in five. Say my cat's hurt or something, then I can zoom home.'

Lucy did what she was told and Maisie made her excuses and left, with Roger promising to contact her about a 'next time', not that Maisie was going to have a next time.

Maisie's next match initially looked promising. Phil seemed well-travelled, well-adjusted to living on his own and he liked cats and dogs. He owned his own home, drove an OK kind of company car, he was slim, reasonably attractive in a Dennis Waterman kind of way – not a look that usually turned her on but she didn't object to it – and dressed well. He'd obviously thought about his burgundy shirt and dark jeans before he'd put them on and she appreciated the effort he'd made. He had also taken the trouble to book a table at a restaurant near the pub where they met and, while he didn't offer to pay for her, she didn't expect it on the first date. Of course, it was always nice to be treated, because somehow it made you feel more special, but it wasn't necessary.

Despite the fact that he worked in insurance, which Maisie knew nothing about except that her car insurance company had driven her round the bend when she'd tried to make a claim recently, conversation hadn't dried up once during the entire evening and Maisie left him feeling excited.

Lucy had said recently that she was now in the car boot sale of life where men were concerned but just occasionally you could snap up a real treasure. Maybe this was her Flog It! moment, Maisie pondered, as they agreed to meet the following weekend and phone one another in the meantime.

Which they did, and chattered on reasonably easily for half an hour. It was a little strained, she thought, but not too bad and she was looking forward to her second date. This time they agreed to meet at another pub where they could eat but as the evening wore on, Maisie detected something uncommitted about him. Fair enough that he never wanted to marry again after having his wife leave him for another woman, but he wasn't up for adventures, either. He said his days of having holidays that involved exciting things like cycling through Vietnam were long gone and all he wanted now was a quiet life. She'd heard that one before and what it meant was that a man wanted a woman who wasn't going to argue with him, nag him or demand too much. In other words, a woman who was going to do everything for him and be a bit of a doormat. She went home feeling downhearted but prepared to give him one last chance.

Now that it was summer, Gus was spending most of his days and much of the night outdoors, hunting for mice which he brought in for Maisie now and again. Occasionally he ate them – she had once, revoltingly, seen him bite the head off one and chomp slowly down its body as she watched him, finally sucking up the tail into his killer mouth like a particularly delicious piece of spaghetti. Then he'd rudely spat the gall bladder out at her feet. 'That's my bit, boy, is it?' she'd said. 'Well, thanks a bunch.'

But tonight, as she got ready for her third date, he was indoors watching her. Maisie stroked his silken head and said, 'I've told Lucy I might ring her if Phil gets too boring – he's in the last chance saloon. I'll use you as an excuse again. You have many uses, little big cat.'

Tonight – again – they were meeting at a pub and tonight – again – Maisie expected she'd be paying for her own meal. It was getting expensive, going out with him, and she had rather hoped he might offer to pick her up before taking her off to a nice restaurant. He showed no inclination to do so, though, and so she in turn felt too insecure to make any move towards him. When they talked on the phone recently she'd realised it was becoming hard to find something in common to chat about and she was rather dreading the evening to come.

Sure enough, conversation dried up early on, after Phil had told her he couldn't be bothered to go on holiday after the latest security scares because it might mean he had to queue to get into the airport.

'This is *so* not going to work,' said Maisie, nipping out to the loo to ring Lucy and put Plan A into action. 'The guy has no zest for life whatsoever. His get up and go has completely got up and gone!'

Lucy's call duly came and Maisie made her

excuse about a sick cat and, without arranging a further date because she knew neither of them wanted one, zoomed back to Cuckstone. It did occur to her as she drove home that she might be tempting fate with her excuses but she dismissed that as fanciful nonsense – something she was skilled at. If it could be imagined, Maisie would imagine it, which was why when the predictable thing happened she was always surprised. She drove straight to The Bell and had a riotous evening regaling everyone with her dating agency disasters. Staggering back home at midnight, a little unsteady on her feet, she started calling Gus, who, unusually, hadn't come downstairs to greet her.

'Oh there you are,' she said, spotting him where he shouldn't have been, roosting on one of the pillows on the spare bed. She stroked his back lightly and was astounded to hear him growl at her. 'What's the matter? Are you hurt?' He growled again. His eyes looked feral, like Saddam's used to, not filled with love as they usually did.

'My God, you are hurt. Let me feel your back, I'll be gentle.' Drunkenly but tenderly she worked her way down his back but he slithered away and poured himself off the bed, moving in a low, fluid fashion quite unlike his usual confident gait. Maisie was too slow to stop him as, keeping himself long and close to the ground, he scuttled down the stairs and slipped through the cat flap. 'Come back, come back, you silly cat, I'll look after you,' she cried, but he was gone.

Maisie ran into the garden with a torch. Eventually she found him crouched far back under her neighbour Sue's huge camellia bush but he wouldn't come out. She must have hurt him when she was trying to find out what the matter was, she realised, cursing herself and her stupid, insensitive drunkenness, and now he was afraid of her. He'd come in for help because he trusted her to look after him, and she'd failed him.

After lying on her stomach in the dewladen grass for more than half an hour, trying to smooth-talk him into coming in, Maisie gave up and went inside. Gus would be back, she was certain. He'd come in by morning for his breakfast and all would be well. She staggered off to bed and conked out but at 5am she awoke, sure something awful was wrong.

'Gus, where are you?' she called but he was nowhere to be seen. By seven she was getting really worried. He'd never stayed out all night before and he wasn't under the camellia bush any more. What had happened to him? Was he much more badly hurt than she'd first thought? Could he have been hit by a car? But he never went on the road, surely that couldn't be the cause of whatever was wrong.

She pulled on some clothes and set off around the allotments, the footpaths and the haunts she knew he loved to visit, searching for more than an hour. It was a beautiful morning but it might as well have been a grey winter's day for all the impact it made on Maisie. She climbed over the padlocked gate into the allotments, ripping her jeans in the process, and proceeded to lift every tarpaulin and look into every cranny she could find. But there was no sign of Gus.

Returning home exhausted, she knocked on Sue's door to ask if she could look in her shed.

'I saw him here at about 11 last night when I got home,' said Sue. 'He was fine – waiting for you, I thought, and when he saw me he ran up the alley and disappeared into your back garden. He wasn't moving in a strange way at all. You know what he's like, I speak to him and he just turns tail and runs.'

Strange, thought Maisie, he obviously hadn't been hurt then. She went over to see her neighbour on the other side. Gus loved

June's garden – it was wild and overgrown and host to a thousand birds, a million mice and the odd rat, the perfect playground for a pussycat. As she poked around in the bushes she knew that he could be within feet of her at any time but if he didn't want to be found, he wouldn't show himself. All she could comfort herself with was the thought that he'd come home when he was good and ready.

Suddenly she heard a voice. Leaning out of a first-floor window was Peter, who lived in June's bedsit. 'You're up early,' he said. 'Have you lost something?'

'I'm trying to find that darn cat. I think he's hurt,' Maisie replied. 'I'm terrified he might have run under a car or jumped off something and hurt his back.'

Peter pushed the window further open. 'I heard a terrible cat fight about 11.30 last night. It didn't last long but there was some frightful yowling going on. It sounded like one of them had really hurt the other. Could it have been Gus?'

Maisie thought for a second. She wasn't aware of any recent feline arrivals in the village trespassing on his patch but maybe he did have a new enemy who had taken a chunk out of him. It definitely fitted. It was also good news – far better than if he'd been out on the road, or so she thought.

'Thanks, Pete, that's really helpful. He was definitely moving last night when I saw him, even if it was in a slithery way, so he can't have hurt himself too badly.'

Maisie spent the day doing odd jobs, mowing the lawn and shopping for her niece Sammy's birthday present in her favourite town, Lewes. 'He'll be home by evening,' she thought. 'Then I can find out what the problem is and call the vet.' But he wasn't. And he wasn't there the next morning when she woke up to get ready for a picnic on the beach with two friends and their three boys. She was really worried now. What on earth could have happened to him? Was he too badly hurt to struggle home and sitting somewhere just waiting to die? Her imagination, vivid at the best of times, ran riot as she sat at her computer typing out a notice.

LOST

Have you seen my beautiful black cat? He's got green eyes, chocolate-tinged fur and has been hurt in a fight with another cat. He may be sheltering in your greenhouse or shed. Please, please

check all outbuildings and if you find him, or you see a cat that fits his description, ring me immediately on the number below.

Then she printed off six copies and raced out to pin them on all the signposts and stiles in the vicinity.

With a heavy heart, Maisie grabbed her coolbox full of picnic food, her portable barbecue, rug and swimsuit and bundled everything in the car. She'd been so looking forward to spending the day with the boys but now she was worried and exhausted through lack of sleep.

As usual, though, the boys were so wonderfully boisterous and enthusiastic about everything that they helped her forget her troubles. Maisie had managed to forget the firelighters, so the first hour was taken up searching for tiny, dry bits of kindling which they somehow managed to get to light and burn the charcoal.

'He'll come back, don't worry yourself sick about a cat,' said everyone, but she wasn't so sure. Gus had never gone missing before. She didn't know how he behaved in a situation like this. What if he was gone for good? How would she feel, not having a cat again? The very thought of it made her eyes fill up with tears. If only she'd been sober on Friday night she'd have dealt with the situation differently and wouldn't be in such a state now. And why did she tempt fate twice by using him as an excuse? She prayed silently to God that if he returned Gussie intact she'd never do that again.

At six o'clock she said goodbye to her friends and headed for home. Surely he'll be there when I get back, she thought. He *has* to be. But he wasn't. Maisie slumped on the sofa, her mind racing. She simply didn't know where to look now, or what to do, so she turned on the telly and sat there steeped in depression. Gus had come to mean so much to her, what if she'd lost him for good? What if he was dying of his wounds in a dark, dank hole somewhere? What if a fox had got him and finished him off? What if, what if, what if...

She went to the kitchen to make herself a cup of tea and as she passed the dining table, a slight movement caught her eye. He was there! Curled up on the chair in the corner, half hidden by the tablecloth, it was his new favourite hiding place. Maisie hardly dared move. 'Gussie,' she whispered, 'Gussie, are you OK?' She tiptoed across to his chair and he looked up at her. His eyes were glassy and he looked scared. She reached out slowly towards him, her hand shaking slightly. Surely he'd let her touch him now, if he'd come back to her?

But Gus evaded her hand, ducking round it and sliding off the chair and onto the floor, scuttling with that same stealthy, spider-like movement towards the kitchen. God, did I lock the catflap? thought Maisie. Oh no, I didn't – and he's escaping. She saw the rear end of her cat disappear. He'd gone again. How could she have been so stupid? She should have locked it, then she could have kept him indoors.

Maisie knew now, though, that having returned home once Gus would probably come home again. Maybe he had just been testing the waters. Although he wasn't his old self, he couldn't have been that badly hurt or he wouldn't have been able to jump on and off the chair. I just have to wait until he returns, she thought, telling herself to be patient, although patience had never been one of her strong points.

It wasn't until the following afternoon that she caught sight of him again. He'd jumped onto the garden wall and was miaowing for her. He clearly wanted to be heard and seen and when she approached him cautiously, he allowed her to rub his ears. Her joy was brief, though, for Gus then slid down the wall and off across June's garden. Gone AGAIN, she thought. Bummer. How on earth can I get him into the house and trap him?

She went indoors and rang Helen, who was the village's unofficial advisor on anything to do with small animals.

'What shall I do?' she wailed. 'Gus won't come home and I know he's hurt. How can I catch him? And even if I do, how will I get him to a vet? I'll never get him into a cat basket and he's terrified enough already.'

Helen told her to keep calm. 'Ring Vets in a Van,' she said. 'They'll come out to you to treat your animal in its own home and they are really nice. I'm sure he's just been bitten in a nasty place and has got an abscess or something. It will need treatment but I doubt if he's got any broken bones, not from the way he's behaving. Now go and lock that catflap, Maisie, so if he does come in he can't escape, and if you do manage to shut him in a bedroom or somewhere, ring me and I'll come up and see him.'

Maisie did as she was told, then started the ironing. She usually put it off indefinitely but tonight it was a displacement activity to help her forget her worries. She was about halfway down the teetering pile of crumpled clothes when she heard a faint noise of paws and claws tapping on the tiled floor. Just stay here, she told herself, don't go out again and frighten him, but after 10 minutes she could bear it no longer and quietly tiptoed up the stairs. Gus was fast asleep on her bed. She pulled the door to and lassooed it tight shut with a stretchy rope. No matter what he did now there was no escape. He was safe at last. Then she went to ring Helen.

Litter tray under one arm, a heavy bag of cat litter under the other, Helen arrived 15 minutes later. 'You'll need these if you're going to keep him indoors for a while,' she said. 'He'll hate it but he was probably house-trained by his previous owners. I expect it'll come back to him.'

She crept in to see the sleeping cat, who immediately awoke and crept under the bed. Helen peered at him from the other side. 'He can't be too bad if he's moving like that but I still think you ought to phone the vet,' she said. 'Cats can be in a lot of pain and not show it like humans do. It's best to be on the safe side and get him checked out.'

Maisie made an appointment for first thing the next morning and then took Gus up a bowl of water and another of his favourite food: tuna fish in shrimp jelly. He hadn't eaten for almost four days, yet he showed no interest at all. His nose was warm and dry and she was sure he had a temperature, which meant that whatever had happened to him was poisoning his system.

Sleep eluded her that night, as she tossed and turned in the back bedroom, worrying about what was happening to her cat. Looking a total wreck by morning, she checked on Gussie, then opened the door to the vet. She gawped as he introduced himself as Tom Brackley. He was gorgeous, with those friendly, chunky good looks she was a sucker for, unruly brown hair and twinkly blue eyes. Closing her mouth, she pulled herself together, explained what had happened to Gus and took Tom upstairs.

Tom managed to extract the cat from under Maisie's bed and then got her to hold his front half while he examined Gus.

'That's the problem,' he said, 'a huge abscess. He's been bitten very badly near the base of his spine, on his bottom. He must have got into a fight and tried to flee and the other cat then sank his fangs in. The wound's filled with poison. I reckon he came in to get help, you know. He must be in a lot of pain.'

Tom touched the swelling and it burst instantly. The stench of pus was overpowering and Maisie felt herself gag as Tom gently washed out the wound with hydrogen peroxide.

'Brave little cat,' she said, stroking Gus's head. 'You're so brave.' Gus was struggling but not that hard. She guessed he was weak from lack of food and the toxins in his system but it must have stung like crazy. Then Tom gave him a huge injection of painkillers and antibiotics.

'That should sort him out,' he said. 'Now leave him in here with the litter tray, his food and water. He needs to be kept in for at least five days and he needs to be kept quiet. He'll sleep a lot and he'll be very nervous for the next few days but he should come round. Then he'll probably rub himself up against you a lot. Cats have a lot of nerve endings in the side of their faces and they stimulate the endorphins – the body's natural painkillers. Just stroke him gently on his face and let nature do the rest. Would you like me to come back tomorrow morning and take another look at him?'

Maisie nodded. Anything to see this wonderful man with the healing hands again. And there was no wedding ring on those healing hands, she'd noticed. That doesn't mean anything, she reminded herself. Some men don't wear rings and others take them off on purpose. Remember Dylan? He wasn't wearing a ring when he first met her but when their friendship threatened to turn into a serious affair – on her side at least – it suddenly appeared and he confessed to being happily married. He told Maisie it had been 'in the jewellers', he hadn't meant to mislead her. She hadn't believed a word of it. How could she find out if Tom was married or not? She had to know.

PAWNOTE: The bottom-biter got me. No cat has ever bitten me in such a place before. My pride is in tatters and I blame it on my mistress. If she'd been at home in bed like I expect her to be at night, it would never have happened but she had gone out leaving me with a particularly unpleasant plate of cheap cat food. Usually when she's at home I make my disappointment clear by racing around. I put on my concrete paws so I'm as noisy as possible and I bolt up the stairs as fast as I can and dash into the bathroom, where I leap into the bath and up onto the basin. It

138

is particularly gratifying if I've come straight in from the garden with muddy paws. If that doesn't get a result I resort to scratching the new stair carpet. This always works and she starts shouting, 'Gussie, stop that RIGHT NOW,' but there's no point putting all that effort into it when she's not here.

Because I was hungry and, I must admit, a little worried about her being so late, I went to wait outside on the front path to greet her. Then Her Next Door came in. She's always been nice to me but this time she addressed me while I was sitting in the alley and that makes me run, even if it's my mistress who is doing the talking. That alley is mine and mine alone and it's a place for quiet contemplation. It's dark and cool, with a refreshing breeze blowing up the middle of it that ruffles my thick pelt and calms me down. I hide behind the recycling bins, where I can see down to the road, so whoever or whatever comes up the path won't take me by surprise. If I look the other way I can see into the two gardens, so anything coming over the back wall is in full view, too. Anyone who ventures in my alley is trespassing and I refuse to give them the time of day.

Anyway, my mistress still didn't come home and I was bored, so I went looking for mice. There was a full moon, the stars were out and it was a lovely night for hunting. I was just hanging around the secret garden on the other side, listening to what might be crawling around in the undergrowth and enjoying the peace when Bam! A huge ginger tom appeared in front of me, yowling. I stood my ground and yowled back but I could see I was in for a pasting. I bared my fangs, hissed and growled but the ginger tom stood his ground and then sprang.

We locked claws and paws, spitting and caterwauling as we tried to rip each other's ears and noses but I knew I would lose. He was younger than me, fit and feisty with hefty muscles and a full set of tackle fuelling his testosterone. As we let go of each other I slowly, carefully backed off, one paw at a time. I didn't turn until I was sure he had understood that I had given in and was no threat to him, even though it was he who was in the wrong and trespassing on my territory.

Believing I was safe I turned my back and went to jump over the garden wall and run to safety in my home. It was a stupid move. He sprang again, biting me hard and deep on my bottom and just missing my spine. It was agony – and of course, utterly humiliating. I let out a howl of outrage and pain and ran for my catflap. I slithered slowly upstairs and hid on the soft and comfy pillows in the upstairs bedroom until she came home. I trusted her to help me but instead she hurt me, pawing me with her great mitts and insisting she had to find out where I was injured. I slipped out of her grasp and ran away. It pained me to run but I knew it would hurt more if I stayed.

On my own once again, I returned to my old haunts, the places I'd frequented when I was a stray – the dark garden shed filled with rubbish, the cave under the tarpaulin on the allotments, the back of the compost heap amidst the crisp, dead leaves. Many times I heard her calling as I licked my wound and waited for the pain to subside but it only got worse. If she got too close I'd wait for her to go and then move again to a new safe place. I missed her but when I did go home she looked as if she was about to poke and prod me again and it seemed safer to leave.

After what seemed like a very long time, day started blurring into night. I realised I was very ill and if I was to survive I had to return home and risk her clumsy hands. She shut me in her bedroom and called a man in to help me who caused me a lot of pain, but then there was relief. I can't remember

141

much of that time – a deep voice and strong hands holding me tightly, an agonising stinging in my wound, the smell of poison and to my shame, my own urine, a prick in my neck between the shoulder blades ... and then the pain seemed to blur away and I slept.

When I awoke I was on my own but I knew where I was. I could smell my mistress's nightie which she'd left on the floor next to me and it brought me comfort. I could hear her snoring in the next room and I could at last crawl to my dishes to eat and drink. The pain had subsided, though I could barely move my back legs. Then I must have slept again.

Now I am confined to her bedroom with nothing to do and no mischief to make and I'm bored stiff. Worst of all, I have to do my business inside, in a litter tray. I haven't used one of those since I was a kitten and think I may die of shame. There are no secrets left between us now.

Chapter Seven

Love is in the Air

At 9am precisely the next morning, Maisie's doorbell went. She had been up for hours – not dressed, mind you, because she was dithering over what to wear. A dress was too dressy, shorts were a definite no with her legs, her only nice jeans were in the wash ... In the end she'd settled for a floaty cotton skirt in jade green and a clean white T-shirt.

She'd spent the first hour of the day with Gussie, trying to entice him out from under the bed. He was better, she could tell. He'd eaten some of his tuna fish in shrimp jelly and he was reaching out for her fingers as she felt under the bed, wanting to be stroked. He'd even used his litter tray, which he must have found hugely undignified for such a private animal. Maisie found it amazing he could even perform a bodily function, given he hadn't eaten or drunk for days.

She had tried to choke down a piece of toast but was too nervous to eat and was peering out of her office window waiting for Tom the vet to arrive when she spotted the distinctive green four-by-four with its white lettering pull up outside. He's as gorgeous today as he was yesterday, she thought, peering discreetly over the window ledge as she watched him walk up the path. Now, how do I discover his marital status? I must be tactful...

With a great deal of coaxing, Tom eventually lured Gus out from under the bed, examined him and declared that he was doing well. 'The wound on his back will need washing out regularly with warm salty water,' he said. 'Just wet a piece of cotton wool with it and dab it around the wound. It'll help remove any residue of pus and keep it clean. It shouldn't heal over just yet anyway or it'll trap any poisons inside.' Maisie didn't think Gus would relish being wetted with anything but she said she'd give it her best shot.

'You're much brighter today, boy, aren't you?' said Tom. 'If I had a cat, I'd like one like you. You really are a beautiful beast.'

Maisie seized her chance. 'Do you have any pets of your own?' she asked.

'Yes, a portly but very naughty Cardigan-shire corgi called Tosca,' he said. 'You know the breed – they've got big pointy ears and long, waving tails and are longer and more thickset than Pembrokeshire corgis, which for some reason are more common.'

A corgi ... that's a funny kind of dog for a man, thought Maisie. Then she realised she'd said it out loud and blushed but Tom didn't seem fazed.

'It's not a breed I'd have chosen,' he said. 'I'd always choose a mongrel. Too many pedigree dogs today are too interbred and the breed standards have done dreadful damage – I see the suffering caused by it all the time. Corgis, for instance, often have appalling back problems because they're bred to be too long and their spine can't cope with it. I had a patient who was the most handsome Cardi corgi I've ever seen and who had the most joie de vivre of any dog I've ever met and he had to be put down at six because he became paralysed from a back problem. It broke his owner's heart.

'The only reason I've got Tosca is because her mistress had to go into a nursing home and I promised her I'd look after Tosca as if she was my own. I've had her for four years now and although she's nine, she behaves just like a puppy. When I take her for walks in the country she always runs off after rabbits and squirrels. She once put up a deer and still remembers exactly where she found it although we only go to that place about every six months. And she's a brilliant footballer and great with kids. I can't believe how much character there is packed into one chunky little dog!'

He obviously loves that dog with a passion, thought Maisie. I wonder if he could love me like that, too? But she was being premature, as usual.

'So who looks after Tosca when you're out and about with work?' she asked, her heart in her mouth. She knew, she just knew that with her luck he was going to say it was his wife and that would be the end of that.

'Tosca goes to a dog minder in the daytime,' said Tom. 'It was easier when I was married but my wife and I split up two years ago and now I'm on my own it's a bit of a juggling act. I can't leave her in the van when it's hot in case the poor dog fries and I can't take her in to see patients with me for obvious reasons. Talking of which, I must tear myself away and get to my next appointment. I'm afraid I need to give you a rather hefty bill – unless you have pet insurance?'

Maisie didn't, although she had every intention of getting some very soon when she saw the size of Tom's bill. The call-out charges alone were almost £100 and the injections and ointments came to another £70. But Gus was worth it – apart from large bills for posh cat food he'd never cost her a penny, and she didn't begrudge the vet's fees for a second. Anyway, she now knew Tom wasn't married and that was news money couldn't buy.

'Shall I pop by in a couple of days and check Gussie out for you?' he asked as he turned to go. 'I'm only in the next village, so there'll be no extra charge. I'd like to see if he's healing like he should. Just keep him indoors until then, he mustn't get dirt in that wound.'

Maisie managed to splutter, 'That'd be great, thanks so much,' as she shut the door behind him. 'Yes, yes, YES,' she shouted, jumping up and down, 'RESULT!' She looked out of the window. Tom was gazing at the door in bemusement but he was smiling. He'd clearly heard her. 'Oh no, how embarrassing,' whispered Maisie.

For the next two days, Maisie's head was in the clouds. She was trying to write an article on creating the perfect kitchen for a national magazine but it was taking a lot longer than normal. When she tried to write about kitchen worktops, her mind kept re-enacting that scene from the movie *The Postman Always Rings Twice,* where some very saucy stuff takes place on a kitchen worktop, substituting Tom and herself for Jack Nicholson and Jessica Lange. Gussie, meanwhile, was recovering well and making desperate bids to escape from his bedroom prison every time she went in there. In the end she relented, blocked up the cat flap and wrote notices to put on the front and back doors reminding herself not to let the cat out. When she opened the bedroom door to release him from his confinement, he peered down the stairs with disbelief, then slowly and rather creakily walked down them. A good sniffing of every skirting board, floorboard and chair leg was in order and when he'd finished he curled up on his favourite kitchen chair and went to sleep.

His wound was healing well and he was surprisingly malleable when Maisie went to wash it twice a day with the warm, salty water that Tom had recommended. It was still oozing a pink-tinged, viscous liquid but was closing up gradually. It was deep, though – Maisie reckoned it had almost hit his spine. A few millimetres to the left and goodness knows what would have happened to him. If she ever got her hands on the cat that had done it to him he would regret it.

After all her bad experiences in the past when men had promised to ring and then never had, Maisie hadn't really expected Tom to call when he said he would. But as promised, two days later the phone went and he arranged to pop over to check on Gussie that evening.

It was about 6pm when he walked up the garden path with his black bag full of instruments, liniments and pills. He didn't look as if he'd been running around looking after sick animals all day, Maisie thought, he looked as if he'd just stepped straight out of the shower.

'Hi Maisie,' he said. 'Nice to see you again. How's that poor punctured pussycat?'

Gussie, as it happened, was hiding under the table in the kitchen, having found for the umpteenth time that there was no escape through the catflap. He'd recognised Tom's voice and now associated it with pain, despite the fact that Tom had probably saved him from a slow death by septicaemia.

'The thing about animals is that you can't afford to give in to their fears,' Tom told Maisie. 'Let them get away with it and they'll continue to manipulate you. Gus has nothing to fear from me as you know, and over time he'll probably learn that, too.'

What did he mean, 'over time'? thought Maisie. Did he mean he was going to be around for a bit? Or did he just expect to make lots more vets' visits over the next few years to this troublesome cat?

'Gus is looking good. You could let him out but leave it until tomorrow morning, when you're here to keep an eye on him,' said Tom. 'He'll probably be quite frightened at first and stick close to home. He's had a nasty scare on top of everything else, so he won't wander far, although I expect he'll forget what happened after a few weeks.'

'Oh, I'm here tonight actually,' said Maisie. 'I could let him out now and watch him.'

Tom looked at her. 'Actually, I was wondering if you'd like to go out for a drink, Maisie,' he said. 'You were my last call so I've finished work now and I'm parched. Could you take pity on a thirsty vet and let him drag you to the pub for a pint?'

'Oh, I suppose so,' said Maisie, nonchalant on the outside but bubbling with excitement inside. 'Got nothing better to do.' She winked at him as she said it. 'No, I'd love to, just let me grab my bag and I'll be with you.'

She nipped in to say goodbye to Gus. 'Bye

for now, be good,' she said, as she always did. 'I'll be back later. And guess what, Gus? I'm going for a drink with Tom! Aren't I the lucky one?' Gus's only response was to stalk towards his litter tray, with a filthy look at her to leave him alone and let him have some privacy.

The Bell's pretty back garden, strewn with ancient apple trees, was more or less empty that night. Tom bought Maisie a drink and they settled themselves down in a secluded corner and began to chat. Why is it, she thought, that when you feel comfortable with somebody, talking to them about almost anything isn't hard work but when you're not at ease then talking about the simplest things is difficult? Tom was really easy to talk to and it wasn't all one-sided. He talked about himself, too. About how he'd got married in his late 20s, how he and his wife Barbara had grown apart rather than together as they pursued their careers, about how he'd wanted children and she hadn't. Then, when she finally decided at the age of 39 that she did want kids, she couldn't conceive. And after all kinds of invasive tests to both of them, it was found to be Tom that had a dodgy sperm count, possibly the result, the doctors said, of a bout of childhood mumps.

The news had forced them even further apart, each going into their shell to cope with the pain of losing what they'd dreamed of. Eventually Barbara had an affair with a Swiss guy – he was called Wiener or something unfortunate like that – who was working as a tennis coach at her gym. Wiener was only in his 20s and when Tom had found out, they'd decided the time had come to divorce. There wasn't even enough love left between them for either party to be particularly acrimonious towards the other, but to be cuckolded by someone so much younger had dented Tom's male pride terribly, particularly coming on top of finding out that he was sterile. It was that, more than the actual divorce and losing the big Edwardian house that they'd renovated together and shared for so long, that had kept him licking his wounds for the last couple of years, during which time, he told Maisie, he hadn't gone out with anybody, let alone had sex with them. Now 45, though, he said he felt ready to enter the fray again.

Maisie had to take herself to the loo at that point, she felt so overwhelmed by events. How come her luck seemed to have changed all of a sudden? Surely she couldn't have found a man who was (a) normal (b) single

(c) good looking (d) intelligent (e) employed and (f) actually wanted a girlfriend! Not all in one male body, it wasn't possible. He would probably turn out to have some absolutely gross habit, like picking his nose in traffic jams or playing pocket billiards in the cinema. Or maybe he'd smack his lips as he ate. An ex-boyfriend had done that and it had driven her mental. When she'd mentioned it he'd refused to speak to her for a whole week. Maybe Tom suffered from violent road rage and turned into a hog behind the wheel. He could even be a stalker or into Internet porn ... the possibilities for fault-finding were endless.

Be quiet, Maisie, she told herself. Don't ruin this relationship before it even is one. You don't know if he's got any of these faults. He might not be fatally flawed. He might be faithful and true, honest, kind and funny, strong and courageous – the sort of man, in fact, that you've been after all your life. Go back outside and carry on finding out who he really is.

Maisie returned to their table to find Tom had two menus in his hand. 'Fancy a bite?' he said. 'I'm ravenous. My treat – you've just paid me a squillion, so I think I owe you. I'm going to have the fillet steak, it sounds fab.'

It was a far cry from miserly Marcus and Maisie ordered herself roast chicken with all the trimmings. The conversation turned to food and she discovered that, like herself, Tom loved to cook but he liked to eat even more. 'The trouble round here is that all the pubs have gone gastro and they're so expensive you can't afford to eat out often,' he said. 'Also, I've found the quality is so unpredictable. One day you'll get a decent meal, the next it's crap. Then you send it back and they don't want to refund your money. The other day I had a pork chop that was so tough I could have used it as a lethal weapon. I get far better meals at my friends' houses than I've found in any pub locally.'

'Ah, but have you tried Amberley Castle?' said Maisie. 'The food is a cut above anywhere else in Sussex, I reckon – lots of local produce and a divine setting under the Downs. I took my mum there last year for her birthday and she loved it.'

Tom looked interested. 'Want to go some time, then? I'd love to try it and you could guide me round the menu.'

Want to go for lunch at Amberley Castle with Tom? Maisie couldn't quite believe her ears. Life, suddenly, looked better than it had for many years.

The rest of the evening passed in a happy haze of food, wine and chat. Tom walked Maisie home at around 11pm and as they wandered up the high street he casually put his arm round her. It was risking instant death to walk two abreast up this road but Maisie was too blissed out to care. When they reached her place, he said, 'I won't come in as I have an early start tomorrow. Take care and I'll ring you. Promise.' He kissed her on the cheek, then on the lips. 'Bye,' he said, smiling. 'Thanks for a fantastic evening.'

'Bye,' said Maisie, faintly. She was in heaven.

'Gus, my little friend, I think we are going to have a man about the house,' she told the cat as she came in. 'I have a good feeling about this one.' He just looked at her.

As Maisie lay in bed that night dreaming of Tom she thought she'd never felt so ready for a relationship. The previous week she'd met up with her first love, a man – boy, really, back then – who she had parted from when she was 19, and seeing him again had somehow laid a lot of ghosts. She and Paul had been each other's first love and when she'd gone to Plymouth to start her career as a journalist they'd drifted apart and never got back together. He had been heartbroken, whereas she had been so busy with work and her new life that she'd hardly ever looked back at what their relationship had been about – and had never realised that it was probably the most important of her life so far.

During their lunch, which took on the guise of a whistle-stop tour through the past 20-odd years with them both jostling for air space, he'd said one thing to her that had rung clanging bells in her head ever since: 'We did pack an awful lot into our three years together.' And he was right, they'd never been still for long. Lack of money had never stopped them doing anything, from travelling up and down the country visiting friends to catching a train back from Switzerland via Paris the summer she turned 18. They had shared so much. It put things in perspective for Maisie about Mike the married man, a perspective she'd needed for a very long time. It made her realise that they hadn't shared much at all really, and that their relationship was built on wishes, if onlys and a lot of hot air, whereas her time with Paul had been solid and could have had a real future if only they'd met at a different time in their lives.

With that realisation had come a release from her feelings for Mike, feelings she hadn't known she still had until they'd finally gone. And good riddance, she thought, he'd hung around in her heart messing things up for far too long. 'Begone from my head, too,' she said to herself, 'I've got more immediate things to think about.'

Maisie began to wonder what would happen when she and Tom went to bed. Would she try to keep her clothes on until the last minute, so he couldn't see how flabby her body had become? Her stomach stuck out because she'd given up the gym, she'd been expelled from her Pilates class after falling asleep with boredom and she'd given up on swimming because it was turning her hair to twine. The result was stubborn, dimply cellulite and flabby bits everywhere. Why had she let herself get so out of practice at this seduction lark? And why had she been so lazy about exercising? She dropped off to sleep knowing she only had herself to blame but somehow it didn't seem to matter.

True to his word, Tom rang the following evening to say he'd had a lovely time with her at The Bell and would she like to accompany him to lunch at Amberley Castle that weekend. Afterwards they walked hand in hand over the wild brooks bordering the castle and rambled through the great pines and chestnuts of nearby Rackham Woods. The little village school at Rackham was where Maisie's great aunt had taught during the war and she'd always had a soft spot for the place.

'Will you be my girlfriend, then?' Tom asked, as they drew up at her place later in the day. 'I'm a pretty straightforward kind of guy and I can't bear not to know where I stand. And I do really like you.'

'You do know I'm a few years older than you,' blurted Maisie. 'Don't you want some bright young thing to have...' She stopped, realising she'd put her foot right in it. She knew he couldn't have kids, how tactless was she?

'It's OK, Maisie, I know you're a tiny bit older and it doesn't worry me. Nor do I want some young blonde with a perfect size 10 body and a vacuum between the ears, and as you know, I can't have children, so your age doesn't matter. But it wouldn't matter even if I did want kids. I like the fact you're a woman of the world, you're independent, you've travelled and you've lived a bit. It's all fine by me. Now, do I take it that's a yes?'

Maisie nodded. 'I like the fact you're so

honest. It means I can say what I mean, too, and that's so important to me. I'm useless at playing games and if I tell lies I can never remember what they were and I get so mixed up. I'd love to go out with you. Are you really going to be my boyfriend? I haven't had one of those for years, so you'd better watch out, I've probably forgotten how to behave.'

He leaned over and kissed her. 'Yes,' he said. 'You're stuck with me now.'

It was the easiest relationship Maisie had ever had. They seemed to fit together in every way – mentally, emotionally, spiritually and physically – like they'd been designed to complement each other. They lived only two miles apart, so could walk between their respective houses and lurch home to either. Because they were both busy with work, at first they saw each other mainly at weekends, which they spent walking the highways of the South Downs and exploring the ancient beech woods at their foot with Tosca the corgi. Their favourite place of all, though, was the hill behind Maisie's house which they'd nicknamed Long Hill, because it was so steep. Her office overlooked it and when they sat on top they'd look down at her window and joke about how the view of the hill inspired her to write her words of wisdom.

As Tom and Maisie got to know each other better, more and more of their time was spent together. Friends started inviting them round to dinner as a couple, which at times Maisie found quite hard to deal with. She was fine with it when it was friends who'd always accepted her as a single woman but not so comfortable when it was mates who'd ignored her over the years and now socialised with her because she had a man in her life. She knew they meant no harm but it still made her cross, but then she'd been cross about it for ages.

Generally, though, she wasn't half as cross with life as she had been. It's probably because I'm in love and I'm sleeping with somebody who loves me, she thought. I hate to admit it but there's definitely something in that. Maybe sex sorts out your hormones...

Amazingly, despite all the pain he had been in, Gus had taken to Tom and never showed the kind of proprietorial behaviour he'd displayed towards her previous prospective boyfriends. His wound had taken a couple of months to heal and had left a hard, raised patch in the centre of a shaven area of short, glossy black hair on his backside. He was more docile these days, rarely straying far from the garden, preferring to sit on the garden wall or shed or even the flat kitchen roof, loftily watching the world below go about its business. But he still bolted whenever a dog came to the house.

If Tom was there, Gus would sit beside him on the sofa – never on Tom's lap but snuggled up tight against him. Sometimes, if he could find a gap he'd wedge himself between the two of them and push Tom to one side by stretching out as far as he could go. He wasn't above exerting his position as top cat of the household even now, and he still liked to dominate Maisie's attention, but he didn't feel he had to protect her any more.

Still his first love, he would pop up every night for his evening cuddle and on to her bed again at first light for his morning cuddle. If Tom was there, Gus would jump on the bed, turn round and jump off again, going to sleep outside the door in his basket. But if they were making love, he wouldn't come near the bedroom. Another male pawing his beloved mistress was not something he ever wished to witness.

PAWNOTE: She's happy now. She's found a good man and he's kind to me, too, although I am still determined to be the

161

main male in her life. I grew up in a household where there was a man and wife and I don't object to it in principle but I do expect to be the centre of her attention. If that stops and she begins to neglect me, I shall have to reconsider my position. After all, it's not as if I can really look after myself, is it? I came to her two years ago because I needed her to feed me and protect me from harm, which this summer has proved only too clearly is of great importance to me. I am not invincible, nor am I a young cat who can stand his ground any more. I have to face it, I am a dependent and on her I must depend.

Even though he hurt me, I like the man, although I balk at calling him my master. It's not as if I've chosen him, as I chose her. No, he has manoeuvred himself into her affections but he is better than the other men who have come to this house, and that is about as good as it will ever get. I realise now that I was a very sick cat indeed when he came to help me and although he may have hurt me in the process, I forgive him. He saved my life and for that I will be forever grateful. I do have some spare lives left, though, so I'm not beholden to him in any way.

This last escapade definitely used up one of them. I am on the mend now but it has been a tedious time for me. Confined to quarters, unable to jump long distances without it hurting my wound, banned from the bedroom when the man started to stay overnight, I've seen a change to my quality of life and it's definitely the poorer for it. I've been forced to pace the floor and do even more watching and waiting than usual. My surveillance has taught me very little. I haven't seen the ginger tom who bit me again and I still don't understand what he was doing in next door's garden that night. I shall have to be on my guard from now on. These occasional visitors are more danger-ous than those cats who have a regular beat and I don't want to fall foul of him again. Luckily Scabby Penrith has gone to the great cattery in the sky, so at least I am ultimately victorious in that I have outlived him.

When I was locked in, I had to entertain myself in ways that only indoor cats do and find new places of interest. The bathroom cupboard became a particular favourite of mine when I discovered it opened up to expose a space that runs the length of the bath. This cupboard wasn't always there – it appeared miraculously one week after some

rather noisy men had been in the house –
but I realise now that it must be checked
every day as danger could be lurking under
the bathtub. My mistress has remarked on
the fact there have been muddy footprints
in the bath recently and that is because I like
climbing into it when I come in from the
garden and lapping at the dripping tap. I
also like drinking from her water glass on
her bedside table but she gets cross when I
do that, so usually I wait for her to go to
sleep first. I think she puts different water in
my bowl downstairs because it doesn't taste
the same, so I never touch it.

I do have some complaints about my food
at the moment, which is disappointing after
all the education I have tried to give her. She
cooks herself delicious-smelling meals, even
more so since he's been around, and I'm not
allowed any. Occasionally I sneak up to her
plate and manage to get a lick of whatever it
is she's concocted but usually I'm waved
away. I only want a taste. If she does give me
fresh food – fillet steak, minced lamb,
salmon, Gruyere cheese and my all-time
favourite, the sweet, frothy cream from the
bottom of a chocolate and hazelnut mousse
– I only need a little taste to satisfy my
craving and then I am done. My previous

owners used to give me sweet stuff when they wanted to slip a pill down my throat, so I know not to let her get too close and to scarper the moment I've had enough. Apparently the pills were for worms – as if a cat as regal as me would give houseroom to something as lowly as a worm.

My favourite meal of all is rationed to about one tin per week. She comes back from hunting holding all these rustly bags. How I hate the noise of them, it gets in my ears and disturbs my equilibrium so much that I sometimes have to flee my home. They are on a par with the vacuum cleaner and the hair dryer, both of which cause me to hide in another room with my paws over my ears. I know she's been successful at her hunting if she opens the sparkly tin containing pale pink, fresh-smelling tuna in a shrimp jelly. I hear her say how I'm costing her a fortune with my expensive tastes but I know she doesn't mind. I can eat a whole tin in one sitting and could still find room for more should it be offered, but it never is.

The man is more generous to me with his food – he gave me a taste of his lamb chop the other night which I enjoyed, although he stopped me taking the chop bone off to eat at my leisure on the armchair. Then I heard him say I was getting too fat and these treats would have to stop. My mistress says she will put us all on a diet for the rest of the summer, which is the worst news I've heard all year. They can eat that grass stuff she calls salad but what will I eat? I can see I shall be supplementing my intake with wild mice again but she gets upset if I bring in animals and birds.

She was particularly annoyed yesterday when she had friends round and was cooking on that tin drum that she calls a barbecue in the garden – why, I don't know, because she has a perfectly good cooker in the kitchen. The man was prodding the meat and I decided I'd like to contribute. Recently I've found a new source of fun – baby rats, which infest the compost heap next door and run the gamut of four gardens. I don't go too close to the parents because they have big teeth but the smaller ones are fair game and easy to catch, so I went and found one, killed it with one bite to its neck in professional cat style, and brought it into the garden to show Tom. He needs to know I'm a force to be reckoned with and can hunt as well as he can. I dumped it under the pear tree and she screamed. 'A rat, Tom, he's got a rat.' Then he came up to me, said, 'Good cat,' gave me a perfunctory pat on the head – and threw it in the dustbin. I'd spent ages staking out the rat family to pick off a good one. Honestly, I don't know why I bother sometimes.

Chapter Eight

Cat-astrophe

Maisie had had some very strange things happen to her in her life. Once, many years ago, she'd managed to get stuck in her own sofa bed. She and a friend had been out for the night and they were laughing so much as she put up the sofa bed that she slipped down the back. Her friend said she was going to send Maisie to work the next day in a Pickfords removal lorry and the more they laughed at what she'd done, the more she'd got wedged beneath the bit that folded out, only it wasn't folding anywhere at that point with Maisie stuck in it. Only a hefty tug from a neighbour, resulting in bruised hips, had got her out of that one.

Since she'd been living in Cuckstone she had spectacularly managed to dislocate her shoulder by falling over in the garden. It was midnight and the wine having run out, she'd been on the Madeira – and sticky liqueurs and Maisie didn't mix, although that had never stopped her. She remembered looking at the stairs and thinking if she made it up there she wouldn't make it down again, so it would be better to go outside. But the second the fresh air hit her she felt sick, so she headed for her neighbour's overgrown garden, concluding that if she puked over the wall nobody would notice. Somewhere along the line she'd tripped over her velvet trouser legs and gone smack down on her arm. It had been agony for weeks. Lucy – who took size nine shoes – said that Maisie's size six feet were stupidly small and she fell over when she'd had too much to drink because she was top heavy.

Since Tom had been around, though, Maisie had calmed down. She'd gone off drinking excessively because the hangovers (and the injuries) weren't worth it and had concentrated instead on enjoying her time with Tom. She had been living in her cottage for almost three years now and had finished all the main structural work. The kitchen had been knocked down and rebuilt and on the whole she was delighted with it. A vast improvement on the original, she now had a proper work surface, a decent oven and room to swing a cat, should she want to. She'd never understood that phrase. Who would want to swing a cat? And would any self-respecting cat would let itself be swung? She was pretty sure Gus wouldn't.

The bathroom had also been updated and the leaky porch had been rebuilt and was now more or less watertight. Each job had taken twice as long as she had envisaged when she moved in and had cost her a lot more money than she had intended spending but now, at long last, she'd said goodbye and good riddance to the builders. She still had to say hello to a few decorators but she'd put that off for the moment. The walls could remain pock-marked and streaky for now, she couldn't bear anybody else in the house. The problem with old places, she'd decided long ago, was that they didn't like having things done to them and a new problem always cropped up when work was being done. It all cost a fortune and was making her hanker for an easier place to live.

Then there was the road outside. It had become even busier, the tempers of the drivers more frayed and the fights outside worse than ever. Every day huge foreign lorries thundered through the village and got stuck in the narrow bit of the high street. The other week she'd been wearing bright turquoise trousers, so she'd hardly been difficult to spot, when a lorry had pulled over and scrunched her up tight against the wall of a house in the high street. It was six inches from her nose by the time it pulled away and she was only saved by the front step of the house she was pinioned against. On the few occasions she'd complained to the lorry or car drivers, she'd got a mouthful of abuse. Maisie wasn't sure how much longer she wanted to live in close proximity to such constant aggression and had begun wondering if it was time to move on.

And there was another reason. Although she loved her home it was quite a girlie place and it had begun to feel rather small when Tom stayed. He was a big man who took up a lot of space and there wasn't enough room to get away from each other when he was around. She didn't mind exactly, but to have enough room for a proper wardrobe for his shirts and another chest of drawers to house his undies would have been nice. Instead they were scrunched up with her knickers. So far he hadn't gone to work in her stripy bikini pants but there was always a first time.

It wouldn't solve anything for them to move to his cottage, either. Victorian rather than Georgian, it had lots of corridors and a nice big kitchen/diner in the basement but only two bedrooms, one of which was used as an office. Tom had done it up beautifully in a spare and minimalist way – lots of soft greys and white, with none of the clutter she'd acquired over the years. Maisie supposed that had been left with his wife when the marriage broke up. When she stayed over at Tom's she liked the feel of his house. It was spacious and light, but like hers it was too small for the two of them long term.

And the long term was what they were now thinking about. They'd been together for more than six months, and for the first time in many years Maisie was in love with a man who was in love with her. The more time they spent together, the more they wanted to spend together and they had talked tentatively about letting out both their properties and renting a larger place to share. It would be a temporary measure: if all went according to plan and they could live together happily, they'd sell one property after another and then buy a bigger home to share. But every time they discussed it they came up against one main stumbling block: Tosca and Gus. To date, his dog and her cat had never met one another and Maisie dreaded the day they would have to be introduced. She was sure that if Gus was made to live in the same house as a dog, he would leave home and never return. He'd run away from his owners once, after all, because he didn't want to move house, and he'd sought her out as his new mistress. What was to stop him doing it again?

Tom wasn't so worried. As a vet he knew that cats were fickle creatures and could often – as in the case of Katie and Sky – become top dog, as it were. He thought that given a sensitive introduction and time to get used to each other gradually, Tosca and Gus would rub along fine.

'You know, Maisie, we're just prolonging the agony,' he said to her one day. 'If we don't get on and introduce them, we'll never know if it's going to work or not. We just have to take the plunge.'

Maisie nodded. She knew he was right. 'OK then, let's do it next Sunday. If you drive Tosca over here and bring her into the living room, holding on to her collar so she can't get away, I'll have Gus on the sofa and be sitting next to him, holding on to him so he can't escape. If we just let them sniff one another first from a distance then hopefully Gus won't be too frightened. But you must promise not to let Tosca go. Gus will have nowhere to escape to if you do and he'll be terrified. Then all our good work will be undone and I doubt if Gus will ever give Tosca a second chance.'

She was dreading the encounter and as Sunday came nearer she got a sinking feeling in her stomach that she feared heralded something bad happening. With her the phrase 'gut instinct' was totally accurate. As a little girl, her tummy had been where her guilty conscience resided, just above the belly button, and if she had done something wrong she would get really bad stomach ache which wouldn't go away until she confessed to her crime. Then, when she had grown up, her gut had always told her when a boyfriend had been unfaithful or had gone off her because she suddenly found herself unable to eat in front of him. It was a flaming nuisance because there had been times when she'd rather have turned a blind eye but she always knew and she had never been wrong.

That awful lurching feeling had never happened with Tom but it was there inside her now, like personal aircraft turbulence bouncing around and making her feel unsafe. She'd have done anything to put off the encounter between dog and cat but she knew that it had to come sometime and that without the two animals meeting up, she and Tom couldn't plan their future together – or even a future apart. That was a solution that Maisie couldn't bear to think about.

Tom said he'd drive over with Tosca in the morning and arrive at Maisie's place for lunch, when the introduction was to take place. It was to be brief – just a quick sniff from Tosca to see how she reacted to the sight of a cat at close quarters and to monitor Gus's reaction, which was bound to be extreme. Maisie didn't hold out much hope that anything good could come from the encounter but even she, full of foreboding, couldn't have imagined how bad it was about to get.

When Tom arrived, she was sitting on the sofa with her hands clamped firmly on Gus's shoulders. Tom let himself in with his own front door key. Maisie could hear the scuffle of Tosca's feet as they came into contact with the tiled flooring in the porch and she felt Gus stiffen beneath her. She moved her hands down and held on tightly to his front legs as Tom and Tosca came in slowly. The dog's nose was twitching and when she caught sight of Maisie she pulled forward, tail wagging like a flag in the wind as she made little grunting sounds. She loved Maisie and intended to give her the usual enthusiastic greeting but Tom now had tight hold of her collar. 'Whoa, Tosca, sit down,' he said to her sternly.

Never obedient at the best of times, she ignored him and continued to strain towards Maisie. Then she caught sight of Gussie, who by now was struggling to free himself from the grip Maisie had on his front legs and rolling his green eyes in terror. Uh-oh, this isn't going to go according to plan, thought Maisie.

Tosca lurched forward at the exact moment there was a loud knock on the front door, which swung open, hitting Tom hard in the back. Startled, he let go of her and she jumped at the cat, who wrenched himself free of Maisie and leapt into the air, over the top of the sofa and then over the dog, before running out of the door at full pelt with Tosca in hot pursuit.

'Tom, stop them! They'll get hit by a car,' screamed Maisie, as the pair of them pushed past the man on the door step. It was a neighbour come to collect a parcel she'd taken in for him four days before. Talk about choosing an inopportune moment.

Tom grabbed Tosca's tail as he chased Gus down the path. If only Gus had known it, there wasn't a hope in hell of a portly corgi catching a fit black cat but he was panicking and wasn't going to stop for anyone. Tosca yelped as Tom grabbed her thick tail and ground to a quick halt just as she reached the front gate – but Gus kept on going.

'STOP, Gussie!' yelled Maisie, 'STOP! You'll be killed.'

At that second a black BMW with tinted windows overtook the other cars politely waiting their turn to pull out around Maisie and Tom's parked cars. Revving his engine from a standing start he started to accelerate past them – just as the terrified cat ran out into the road.

The next few seconds seemed to happen in the kind of slow motion Maisie had heard about but never experienced. The shiny chrome bumper of the car collided with the cat, tossing him into the gutter like a rag doll, limbs sprawled awkwardly. Maisie heard the thud, saw him land hard on his left side and lie there in the road – and then everything ricocheted forward again into the present.

'Gussie, oh Gussie,' she cried. 'Oh God, I can't bear to look.'

Tom manhandled his struggling dog into the house, slammed the door and ran to the cat.

'He's still alive, Maisie,' he said.

Blood was pouring from a deep gash in Gus's back leg as Maisie leant over him. His flanks were heaving as he struggled to breathe, his left front leg was stuck out at a funny angle and his tail was bent up like a corkscrew. She reached out to touch him and he looked at her but his eyes looked cloudy and dull. Oh God, Maisie agonised, had she killed her cat all because she was so greedy and wanted to have it all? Thoughts flashed through her mind as she touched his chocolate velvet fur with one finger and he let out a weak growl. He was clearly in distress but just how badly was he injured? Did he have internal bleeding? Was his brain all right?

'Tom, we have to get him to the animal hospital,' she said.

Suddenly there was a burly, bald man looming above her. 'Why can't you people look after your animals properly?' he shouted. 'I could have had a serious accident just now if that dog had run out in the road, too.'

Maisie looked up, tears streaming down her face. 'This is your fault for driving like an idiot, you selfish pig,' she shouted. 'You might have killed my cat.' He jumped back into his BMW and gunned the engine, giving her a V-sign as he roared off, leaving her distraught on the pavement.

Tom tapped her on the arm. 'Maisie, this is no time for hysterics. Stand up and let me look at Gus. We have to get him into theatre and X-rayed to find out the extent of his injuries and the sooner we do that the better.'

Maisie bent over Gus. 'Be brave, little cat,' she said. 'It'll be OK, just hang on in there. You can do it and I'll be with you all the way.'

Tom put a temporary dressing on Gus's bleeding leg and levered a small stretcher under the stricken cat, which he then secured with two straps. 'Quick, jump into your car and follow me in,' he said. 'We'll go straight to the animal hospital in Brighton, they have the equipment we need to deal with emergencies like this. I'll ring them on the way to say we're coming and they need to get the theatre ready. Don't worry too much – I suspect Gus looks worse than he actually is. I'm so sorry, Maisie, this is all my fault for not shutting the door properly.'

'Please, just get him to hospital, Tom,' replied Maisie. 'We can talk about this later.'

Still sobbing she climbed behind the wheel of her Mazda and followed Tom into

Brighton. 'Please God, don't let Gussie die,' she prayed, over and over again. 'I'll do anything – anything at all – if you just let him live. Please don't let him die.'

At the hospital, Tom lifted Gus out of the car and took him straight into theatre for X-rays while Maisie sat in the waiting room. 'I promise not to leave his side,' he pledged to Maisie. 'I am so sorry, this wouldn't have happened but for Tosca.'

Maisie knew it wasn't Tom's fault but she couldn't quite forgive him yet, even though she knew there was really nothing to forgive. Instead she rang Lucy and asked her to collect Tosca and look after her until the current crisis was resolved one way or another. Then she sat there fretting and biting her nails to the quick.

It seemed like hours before Tom returned. 'I can't give you much good news at the moment, I'm afraid,' he said. 'Gus has been X-rayed and is being prepared for surgery as we speak. The injuries we can see aren't life threatening – he has a fractured leg that needs setting and that bad cut in his hind leg which needs stitching – but we don't know if he has internal injuries. We're worried because his gums are very pale, which indicates bleeding, but that may be down to that nasty wound in his leg and to shock. There's also a problem with his tail.

'Now, I'm going in there to assist the vet and together we'll do our absolute best for darling Gus. As soon as I have any news I'll come out and let you know but you might need to prepare yourself for a long wait.'

He leant over and hugged her. 'I think it'll be all right, you know. He's fit and healthy and strong and he hasn't used up all his nine lives yet.'

Maisie paced up and down the waiting room, wishing she still smoked so that she had some displacement activity to take her mind off what Gus was going through. As she grew calmer, she thought back over the three years she'd had him. When he came to her, dirty, dusty and hungry, semi-feral and full of plaintive miaows, she had looked into his eyes and pledged to take care of him for the rest of his days. How was she going to do that if she moved in with Tom? Even if he got through the next few hours on the operating table, Gus would never recover from his terror of dogs now.

She had expected so little when he decided to adopt her but he'd given her so much. He'd snuggled up to her whenever she was sick or sad, he'd brought her numerous presents of live mice and dead birds when she'd been out of action with her dislocated shoulder and he thought she was too injured to hunt for herself. He had been her best friend through all the horrors of trying to find a decent boyfriend and her companion in the sometimes lonely months after she'd moved to the village and had still to make such firm friends with the locals.

Was the answer to give him away to a good home? But how would she know what a good home was? And if she did find one, would he go? He'd refused to leave the area once – what if he did that again and hung around her cottage pining away? Or maybe he'd trek for miles across country, risking his life to return to her. She'd read about cats doing that and she had no doubt it was in him. He did adore her and she knew she couldn't do such a heartless thing to him and live with herself. It was definitely not an option.

Tom on the other hand was her soulmate, the love of her life, so how could she not move in with him? If they were to spend the rest of their lives together, and it was her dearest wish that they would, they had to move in together at some stage, didn't they? She'd spent a whole lifetime waiting to meet him, missing out on having children, struggling to make ends meet when she'd lost jobs or been sacked by yet another egocentric editor. Her friends had said her man would come along when she least expected it and she'd been least expecting it for years and it had still taken ages. She'd learned to live with loneliness and had grown to like her own company but she did not want to go back to being totally alone now, not having found the man she wanted to spend her life with so late on. She was almost 50, for God's sake.

If it's taken me this long to find someone, I'll probably never find anyone like him again, so that'll be the end of it for ever, she thought gloomily.

The only other answer was for Tom to get rid of Tosca but how could she ask him to do that? Tosca was too old to be re-homed and anyway, he adored her, she adored him and it would break his heart, and Tosca's, probably. If she loved Tom at all – and she was passionate about him – how could she ask him to do that? It would be a sacrifice too far, she decided, and she never, ever wanted to become the sort of woman who would ask a man to do that for her.

As Maisie alternately sat on the hard red

plastic chair in the waiting room and paced the cracked vinyl floor, the thoughts went round and round in her head. There seemed to be no solution. Whichever way she turned there was heartbreak and the future looked bleak.

It was hours before Tom finally came back in. He was dropping with tiredness, his eyes bloodshot and his normally tanned face grey. Maisie looked up, her heart in her mouth. 'Good news,' he said, pressing a finger to her lips. 'Gus has no internal bleeding. His front leg has been set – the humerus was broken so we've had to put a pin in – and his back leg has been stitched. Recovery will be slow but Augustus Moon will live to catch another mouse.

'Oh yes... Sorry, there is a bit of bad news but it's nothing serious. We've had to amputate part of his tail – about four inches – and there's a kink in it further down which I don't think will ever straighten up. It won't stop him functioning, though.'

Maisie burst into tears again and threw herself on Tom's shoulder. 'Thank you,' she sniffed. 'Thank you for saving his life. You don't know how much that means to me.'

'It was the other vet really,' replied Tom. 'She's a whizz at putting small animals back together. Maisie, he's going to be out of it for a while now and there's no point you waiting around worrying. I think you should go home and come back later in the morning, when you've had some sleep. You can see him then.'

By the time Maisie had got herself together and left the hospital, dawn was a faint glimmer on the horizon. She drove home slowly, crawling over Ditchling Beacon instead of driving in her normal bat-out-of-hell mode. She pulled into the car park on the top of the Beacon and watched the sun come up. Gus with only half a tail? How would that work? Maisie couldn't imagine how he'd cope, it would have lost all its whippiness. He'd never again whack her with it if she talked too much or use it to help himself leap huge distances, or just do his funny welcome with it shivering away at her when she came in from work. But he was alive and despite his injuries, he would mend. Her gorgeous cat was going to be OK.

As another beautiful morning dawned, she watched the sun burn off the mist as it rose in the valley below but there was no answering glimmer of light in her own life. Maybe there was a solution to the problem of Gus and Tosca but she was too tired to see one.

She got back in the car and wiggled her way down the bends of the Beacon to her cottage. She'd sort it out with Tom later but right now, after all the trauma of that terrible Sunday, it was the comfort of her bed that beckoned.

PAWNOTE: Where am I? The pain is agonising and that man, Tom, is standing over me and prodding me. I can hear my mistress crying but I can't see her properly, my eyes have gone blurry. I'm being lifted onto a piece of wood but everything hurts so much and it's all going black...

When I come to, there are lots of bright lights around me and some terrible chemical smells that get up my nose and scream 'vet' at me. I hear soothing voices and I try to move away to a place of darkness and safety but someone says, 'Steady, old boy, you're OK,' and strokes me softly on the face. I'm frightened, where is my mistress? She said she'd never leave me and I need her now and she isn't here. She should be with me in times of trouble. There's the sharp prick of a needle in my neck and I start to feel very sleepy but I must stay awake if I'm to stay safe. Then I hear the whine and the whirr. It's that terrifying thing that cuts off my hair and it's on my back leg ... then my shoulder ...then...

I wake in a cage. I can't move. They've put a huge white collar round my neck and it is stopping me turning round to lick my wounds. I can feel tubes sticking out from every part of my body. What has happened to me? Where is my mistress? I miaow and miaow and eventually somebody comes and I hear them say, 'He's awake and he's not a happy boy,' and they rub my ears very tenderly. It's soothing but I'm so frightened. What has happened to me? What is going to happen to me next? I've heard tales of animals going into these places and never coming out alive again.

I shudder and whimper as I remember a dog – a slavering animal with ivory fangs, a long pink tongue like a slice of uncooked bacon and lots of black and white fur – chasing me out of the house and down the path and into the road, a place I learned many years ago never to go. There was a bang and I was thrown up in the air and I landed hard in the gutter, then terrible pain and then ... nothing. But where is the woman I love? She should be here by my side. I close my eyes and sleep. Maybe this is the end.

Chapter Nine

The Past Pays a Visit

At what seemed like the middle of the night but was in fact 10am, Maisie's phone rang. She'd been in the deep sleep of total exhaustion but as she came to, she remembered that Gussie was in hospital with drips and drains sticking out of him and she snapped awake, her heart thudding with dread.

'Hello?' she said, expecting it to be Tom with a condition check on the cat.

'It's me,' said the voice at the other end. It was a voice she hadn't heard for a very long time. Mike's voice, her married ex-lover. Once, and not so very long ago, either, she'd have been thrilled to hear from him but now she wasn't so sure. What did he want?

'Maisie, I need to see you,' he said. 'Can we meet up?' Talk about picking your moment, thought Maisie, I really don't need this in my life right now, it's complicated enough already.

'Why?' she stuttered. 'Why are you ringing

me? What's going on? I haven't heard from you for years. Are you ill or something? Have you lost your job?'

'No, nothing like that, but it is important. I can't explain over the phone, it's a bit of a long story. When are you free?'

Maisie felt like saying 'never' but even though she and Mike had parted company years ago she was intrigued. What could he want to say to her after all this time? As a couple, they were dead and buried, weren't they? Anyway, now she had Tom. 'I have a few things on my plate at the moment, Mike, and I'll need to have a think about it and get back to you. What's the best number to get you on these days?'

She wrote it down on the pad she always kept by her bed in case inspiration struck in the night. He'd given her a landline number as well as a mobile, which was strange. What if his wife picked up? Well he must have done that for a reason, she decided. She'd ring him in a few days. For the moment she had more pressing matters to sort out.

She rang Tom first. 'How's Gussie this morning?' she asked, without stopping to ask Tom how he was.

'He's responding well, I was just about to phone you,' replied Tom. 'I've just put down the phone to the hospital and he's come round and is miaowing. They want to keep him very quiet, though, and it may be better if you don't go in and see him just yet. The less he's disturbed the better, and if you make a fuss of him then leave him, he may get upset. Perhaps tomorrow.'

Maisie wasn't happy about this but she could see the sense in it. 'Are you sure he's going to be OK? He had a hell of a knock. How could any cat recover from those injuries?'

'Believe me, Maisie, I've seen much worse and the cat has survived. He'll be sore and stiff for some time but he will recover. It's just a blessing that he doesn't have any internal bleeding, that's what usually kills them – things like a ruptured diaphragm can be really bad. We did think that was what had happened to him but it wasn't the case. Look, I've got to go now, I'm on my rounds. Speak later?'

He rang off, leaving Maisie reassured about her cat's future but not so happy about Tom. He hadn't even apologised, for God's sake, yet the accident was caused mainly by him leaving the door open and failing to control his disobedient dog. If he'd shut the door properly, poor Gus would not now be lying in hospital in agony with half a tail, broken bones and various drips and drains sticking out of him. Tom had known how important it was to get the introduction right between the animals if they were going to be able to plan a future together and he had totally stuffed it up.

As the day wore on, she could feel her anger growing and by the time evening came and Tom still hadn't rung her she was at boiling point. I'm going to call Mike, she thought, and say that I will meet him for a drink to find out what he wants. After all, there's nothing to lose.

She dialled his mobile number, her heart in her mouth. She knew she was doing this partly to spite Tom but she didn't care. 'Mike, it's me. I'll meet you for lunch on Wednesday when I'm in London and we can catch up then. It won't be for long, though. Is that OK with you?' Mike sounded hugely relieved as he confirmed he'd be at the Wine Press in Fleet Street – an old haunt of Maisie's from years back and one which she'd never left sober – at 1.30pm. What on earth did he want from her? He still hadn't said.

Then she rang the animal hospital, to be told that Gus was sleeping and making progress. 'He ate a bit of dinner,' said the nurse, 'which is always a good sign with animals. Why don't you come in and see him tomorrow and we can discuss his after care? Also, I need your insurance details.'

Thank God she'd taken out insurance when Gus got bitten by the ginger tom, thought Maisie. She'd never have afforded this otherwise, she'd have had to remortgage the house. He was worth every penny but this had been an expensive year so far.

Tom didn't ring her that night, which surprised Maisie, but then she didn't ring him, either. Maybe he's feeling guilty, she thought. Men and guilt didn't mix in her experience, they tended to take it out on the person they were feeling guilty about. But she was surprised, Tom had never played games before, he'd never been unreasonable or insensitive. And she was still angry with him; maybe he'd sensed that and decided to lie low for a day or two. She couldn't believe anything was seriously wrong between them, not when it had been so good up until Sunday lunchtime. If he doesn't ring me tomorrow morning, I'll definitely call him in the evening, after I've been to see Gus, she decided.

The cat was a sorry sight, though, and she

was devastated to see the state he was in. Miaowing piteously, he rubbed his face against her hand constantly, releasing the endorphins which would help calm the pain in his broken body. The fur had been shaved off the injured back leg, which was a mass of stitches and had a drain in. The fractured front leg was also bald where the pin had been inserted and again, it was stitched. And his tail ... it was bound in a heavy white bandage and looked half the length it had been the day before. Poor little cat. She sat by his cage for over an hour, crying silently, her face against the cage. What had she done to him? This would never have happened if she had just been content with going out with Tom. It wasn't *that* important that they lived in the same house, they hadn't even been together very long. Now she had a ghastly feeling that everything was ruined and nothing would ever be the same again.

With a heavy heart, Maisie left Gus, promising she'd be back to check on him the next day, although she knew time would be tight because that was when she was meeting Mike.

Tom rang her when she got in. 'Maisie, I'm so sorry I haven't been in touch but I've been frantic. I had a sick Labrador to deal with last night and I was trying to save him. He was just a young pup but he'd eaten a bird with poison in it that must have been left out for a fox – you know what greedy-guts Labs are. I battled for hours to save him but I couldn't and he was in agony so I had to put him down. It was so sad and his owners were shattered. After Gussie the day before I felt too depressed to talk.'

Maisie immediately felt sorry for him – and ashamed of herself for doubting him. He was a good man and he cared so much about animals that it must be heartbreaking to work with them and not be able to save their lives. She didn't know how he and other vets did it.

'Look, Maisie, I owe you a huge apology about what happened. If I'd shut the door properly behind me then Tosca wouldn't have been able to chase Gussie down the path and he'd never have run into the road. I know it was my fault. Can you ever forgive me?'

'I think so,' said Maisie, honestly. 'It wasn't really your fault but I can't quite feel that right now. The vets at the hospital say Gus is doing well, although to me he looked a frightful mess. I feel terrible about it, too. I should never have agreed to the animals meeting like that, it was stupid. What were we thinking of? Well, I can answer that. We were thinking about ourselves, not the animals we're supposed to love. But where do we go from here?'

'I don't know,' said Tom. 'I've been racking my brains, too. I suppose we just go on as we were before. Living together isn't really an option, is it, unless one of us gets rid of our pet and I don't think either of us could live with the guilt if we did that. Oh, there goes my bleep again, got to go. Listen, I'll call you again tomorrow.'

And that decides precisely nothing, thought Maisie. Our relationship will stagnate unless we move it forward but that's the one thing we can't do. She went to bed feeling extremely low. At one time the thought of meeting Mike would have had her shaving her legs and applying facepacks the night before so she looked radiant for him but now she really couldn't give a damn. But the next day on the train to London she felt a little frisson of excitement. What would he be like now? Would he have got fat and bald? Would he be friendly or starchy? She hadn't seen him for at least five years and the last time they'd met had been extremely stilted. It was as if he'd been denying himself the chance to enjoy her company in case she got the wrong idea.

She probably hadn't helped the situation by asking him point blank if he was still happy with his wife, to which he'd replied that he was, thank you. It had all been frightfully formal and to help things along she'd played the clown and laughed her way through the lunch, although she was feeling a very different sort of funny inside. In the end she'd been glad to leave. Since then, until the other morning, they'd rarely spoken except to wish each other the occasional happy Christmas by text message. Now he wanted to see her. What on earth could he want?

She found him in the back of the Wine Press, sitting at a dark table in the corner with an expensive bottle of Pinot Noir, her favourite red wine, already on the go. He poured her a glass without asking and pushed it over to her. 'It's nice to see you, Maisie, thanks for coming,' he said. 'Do you want to eat? I remember how you enjoy your food.'

Maisie nodded. 'Yes, please, it is lunchtime after all and I'm ravenous.'

'Some things never change, then,' he laughed. It lightened the atmosphere between them, which suddenly felt easier. She looked at him properly for the first time. Still the same crinkly blond hair, slightly receding but definitely not reaching slap-head stakes yet. More wrinkles round his treacle-brown eyes, more weight round his middle but then she was the same. Yup, the ageing process had dealt them pretty much the same hand, which was comforting.

Maisie studied the menu and eventually ordered a crayfish and mango salad. She wasn't that hungry suddenly. Seeing Mike was making her feel a bit dithery and she still didn't know what he wanted.

'So, why am I here?' she asked him. 'What have you got to tell me that's so important?'

He took a deep breath and looked straight into her eyes. 'My wife has left me for someone else. We're getting divorced and I'm about to be single again,' he said. 'I've never forgotten you, Maisie. You were always at the back of my mind but I had to stay because of the children. Now they're grown up and I'm on my own. I just wondered if there was a chance ... I mean, I wondered if we could see if there's anything left between us.

'Anyway, how about you? I heard you'd moved to the country. Have you got lots of lovelorn swains chasing you?' He'd done a quick about-turn the minute he'd stated his intentions, which didn't pass Maisie by. He was clearly nervous and worried about a knock-back, she was pleased to note.

'Well,' she said slowly, as she tried to take in his news. 'I've met a lovely vet and have been going out with him for a while now. We've run into a few problems recently but I think it's all going to be OK.' She saw no reason to lie. After all, Mike had kept her waiting for this moment for 13 years and now it was too late. Tom was the man she loved, the man she wanted to spend her life with ... wasn't he?

'Oh,' replied Mike, taking a large glug of wine. 'So you're with someone?'

'Yes, well, things do change,' she replied, crisply. 'It's taken me a long time to find a good man. I've lived on my own with my cat for a while now and I have a good life but there was always something missing. Now I think – I hope – that I have a future with Tom. Anyway, that's enough of me, tell me about you.'

She listened in amazement as Mike told her how his wife had never forgiven him for the affair with Maisie. She'd bided her time until their two girls were old enough to have left home and then she'd looked round for an affair of her own. Eventually she'd gone off with a lecturer from their eldest daughter's university and had told Mike she wanted a divorce. It was the first time he'd realised anything was wrong, so it came as a total shock. That was eight months ago and he'd been licking his wounds ever since. He'd moved out of the family home, which was now on the market, and had been living with a friend for the first few months. Now he'd signed the lease on a flat in London's Docklands, near to the TV company where he worked.

'The daft thing is, Maisie, that I really thought we were fine and that we'd put the past behind us. I've been pretty busy with work – with all this new technology there are lots of new projects on the go at the moment – and I suppose I hadn't paid her much attention over the last couple of years. But I had no idea she was thinking of leaving me, nor that she felt she had to seek revenge for what happened between you and me so long ago. I honestly thought we'd sorted out our problems but it seems I was well and truly wrong.'

He sighed. 'And now it seems I'm wrong about you as well. You're not single, you're happily tied to Tom, I can see. I've probably put you in an awkward position by asking you to come here and then putting propositions to you but I meant what I said earlier. I've never forgotten you and if only I could have changed things in the past then I'd have been with you anyway. Nobody ever meant as much to me as you, not even my wife, but she was the one I married and she was the woman who bore me my girls and you can't take that lightly. When I married her I meant those wedding vows and I'll be honest with you: if she hadn't left me, I'd still be with her. It was comfortable and having rocked the boat once I swore I'd never do it to her again.

'Ours wasn't the most passionate marriage in the world but we had a solid relationship and a friendship – or so I thought. Now we haven't even got that friendship and I've realised it was all a sham. I've been a bit of a mess recently but I've pulled myself together now and that's when I decided to ring you. It took a lot of courage to pick up that phone, I can tell you, but I'm glad I did it. You're here now, after all.'

He smiled at her across the table, his brown eyes twinkling. Oh dammit, thought Maisie, he's still really attractive. She was a sucker for a twinkle, which had got her into this situation all those years before, but this time common sense triumphed. She picked up her glass and finished her wine. 'Mike, I really have to go. I have to interview somebody and I can't do it half cut, which I will be if I drink any more. I need time to think about what you've said. It's all so confusing.'

As she pulled on her white linen jacket, Mike rose. 'Lunch is on me, Maisie. Thanks for coming, and for listening. Will you ring me once you've come to a decision? I'd love to see you again.' He pecked her on the cheek, looking into her eyes. 'Please ring. I know it sounds daft to say it but I've missed you.' He kissed her again, on the mouth this time. 'Please.'

Maisie left the wine bar with her head in a whirl and her lips burning. She didn't really have an interview to go to but it had been a convenient excuse. Why is it, she thought, that men are like that old cliché about London buses? There are none for ages, then you get two at once. Of course she couldn't go back to Mike, it was beyond question that it was over between them, but the little romantic voice in her head had started plaguing away. 'You loved him once, you could love him again. You know you still find him attractive and he's free now. Isn't he the one you've always wanted? And remember: he likes cats and he hasn't got a dog, which would make life easier.'

Then the sensible voice would start up. 'You don't know him any more. He might have changed since you were in love all those years ago. He might not like you any more, you've changed quite a lot since that time. And he can be boring and un-adventurous, he only thinks about work. He'd drive you mad. He might even go off with another woman when he's with you, like he did with his wife. No, Tom's the one, he's reliable, kind and true.'

The little romantic voice would pipe up again. 'But you adored Mike, he was the love of your life long before you met Tom, this is a dream come true. He works in your world, he understands you – Tom doesn't. What are you waiting for?'

As she travelled home on the dirty, crowded train to Cuckstone, Maisie thought she'd be driven mad by the two voices shrill-ing away at her relentlessly. I know, she thought, I'll ask Lucy. She's sensible and she always knows what to do. But first I have a little cat to visit.

Gus seemed brighter that afternoon, not in such pain, and he moved restlessly in his small cage as Maisie whispered her problems to him. It was so sad – his tail was incapable of swishing with irritation at the sound of her voice because it was still heavily bound but she could see him trying to move it around. For a cat who had never been caged in his life and who had rarely been parted from Maisie except when she was on holiday, he was doing extremely well, she thought. But then he was still quite badly hurt. The nurse told her he'd be ready to go home in a few days but they needed to make sure none of his wounds became infected before they released him. With a final tickle of his furry ears, Maisie left him to the attentions of the veterinary staff who'd come to dress his wounds, and made her way back to Cuckstone. The visit to Gus had taken her mind off her troubles but as soon as she walked back in through her front door they flooded back. What on earth was she to do?

Maisie's decision to ring Lucy was founded on Lucy's unerring knack for saying the right thing, especially where relationships were concerned. After her own traumatic and violent first marriage was over she'd become hooked on self-help books, which Maisie found too dry and repetitive but they had really helped Lucy put the past behind her and develop a useful insight into the way people's minds worked.

Relating the turbulent events of the past few days, Maisie told a shocked Lucy about how Gus had been so badly injured and then about the unexpected call from Mike and their subsequent meeting today. 'It's all spoiled with Tom,' she said, petulantly. 'I'm still angry with him and I don't know if I'll ever forgive him for causing the accident. I know I should but I can't, not yet anyway. And now Mike's on the scene again and I'm in such a muddle I don't know what to do.'

'Calm down, Maisie, you don't have to make any decisions yet,' said Lucy. 'You're upset, overtired and overwhelmed. Of course you love Tom and you want to be with him. You'll forgive him, of course you will, just give it a bit of time. He told you he feels awful about it, what more can he do? Mike's just queering the pitch, you've moved on since then. Anyway, I never liked him much, he was always a bit of a flirt, I thought. If I'm honest, I felt he lacked commitment to anyone except himself.'

Lucy's words were like listening to the sensible voice in her head but it wasn't necessarily what she wanted to hear, so the following day Maisie called Viv. Always an old romantic, her advice was that Maisie should follow her heart and go for the man she'd yearned for all these years. These conversations just muddled her even more and she didn't want to ring Mike until she had an answer for him, so eventually she decided to be an adult about it and discuss the whole issue with Tom. The problem was knowing how to approach it.

Despite his apology, their relationship had cooled slightly in the week that Gus had been in the animal hospital. They'd carried on talking on the phone but Maisie had been busy running around visiting Gus and trying to work in between times and Tom had had lots of trying cases to contend with. The upshot was that they hadn't made time to see one another, so on the Saturday – two days before Gus was due home – Maisie told Tom she was cooking him a romantic meal and that she wasn't taking 'busy' for an answer.

When he turned up, an hour late and full of excuses as to how he'd been delayed putting down an elderly cat, Maisie didn't feel that normal surge of delight at the sight of him. She felt vaguely irritated, even though she knew he was just doing his job. She served up the overdone roast chicken with rosemary and pancetta potatoes and they sat in the garden and ate it with a green salad and a bottle of chilled rose. This should be dreamy, she thought, and yet I can hardly eat a thing because I'm so nervous about the conversation I'm about to have with him.

'Tom, I have to talk to you,' she said. 'Something's happened and we need to discuss it.'

He looked up, frowning. 'I know things haven't been too good this week, Maisie, but I'm sure we can get through it. I'm really tired. Do we have to have an in-depth talk about the moans and gripes of Maisie Maddox tonight? I'm not sure I'm up to it.'

She was shocked. He'd never spoken to her like this before. Where had that come from?

'Tom, I need to tell you something important and I want you to listen,' she said. 'I had a call from Mike this week – you know, the married man I went out with 13 years ago. He's split up with his wife.'

She paused. Tom was fiddling with his food. 'So what's that got to do with us, Maisie? It's all in the past – isn't it?'

'Well, yes it is, but it was tricky seeing him. His wife left him for somebody else and ... umm ... he wants me back. You know what I said about Mike after seeing Paul the other month, I told you that I realised it wasn't as important a relationship as I'd once thought and that I was totally, absolutely over him. But seeing him on Wednesday made me feel confused, particularly as you and I seem to have been going through a bad patch this week. I thought if I could discuss it with you it would help.'

She paused. Tom looked furious. 'So you went behind my back and met up with your ex-lover, did you, Maisie?' he said in a cold voice. 'And how would discussing that with me help our situation, exactly?'

'I didn't think I could refuse to see him, Tom. He might not mean much to me now but he was important once. And when he rang, you hadn't even apologised about what happened to Gus and I just wanted to know what was the matter with Mike. He could have been ill, for all I knew. What was I supposed to do? And then when I saw him I felt sorry for him, I suppose. I don't want him, I want you, but you've been so off with me this week I don't know where I stand any more.'

Tom pushed his plate away and stood up. 'I'm going home, Maisie. I thought I'd made it quite plain to you that I loved you. If that's not enough for you then there's nothing more I can do. Let me know what you decide.'

'But I have decided,' she cried. 'It's you I want to be with. I just wanted to talk about it, to dispel all this bad feeling and I thought if I was honest and confessed that there was still something between Mike and me it would defuse it. I didn't mean to make things worse.'

'You're obviously thinking about leaving me for him, Maisie, or you wouldn't have to ask me what I thought,' said Tom. 'I don't like that. It's disloyal and hurtful and to be honest, it makes me doubt that we have a future. Yes, I have been a bit off with you this last week but this business with Gus made me realise just how much you put that cat first and I'm not sure if I can live with that.'

'What about you putting Tosca first?' she yelled. 'Surely that's the same?'

'I'm not going to argue with you any more about this. I think we need to take a break from each other. Let's speak again when you've made your mind up. Hopefully you'll have got this Mike out of your system by then.'

Tom turned and walked out of the garden, down the alley and up the road, leaving Maisie stunned. What a vile week, she thought. She'd tried to do the decent thing and had just made matters worse.

The rest of the weekend dragged by with Maisie trying to make up her mind what to do. If she was to lose Tom, then at least she'd have Mike but did she want him? She owed him an answer, even if it was a no, and anyway, all wasn't lost with Tom. On the other hand, maybe it was. He'd never been nasty to her like that before. They'd had the odd squabble but usually it was niggling little things and whoever was in the wrong would apologise and that was the end of it. This was different and she'd seen a side of Tom she didn't like. She was so sick with worry she couldn't eat.

That old adage about life dealing out bad things in threes so often seemed to come true and on Monday Maisie received another huge blow. This time it was the news that the magazines which had provided her with the majority of her income for the past six years had appointed an in-house editor and her services were no longer required. There would be no money to compensate her for the fact she had been, in essence, made redundant. How was she going to pay the mortgage now?

The only bright spot in a dim day was that,

after a week in hospital, Gus was due home, and Maisie was about to drive into Brighton to pick him up. She was nervous, though, of looking after what was still a very poorly cat. She knew that his drains would be out and his wounds would be healing but she was about to become a full-time veterinary nurse and he was the hardest beast in the world to look after. In just eight days, her life had gone from promising to worrying and the only good thing she cheered herself with as she sat behind the wheel of her car, was that she was losing weight. Almost half a stone down already and her waistbands were loose. There's nothing like the heartbreak diet, she thought, for instant results. Shame it's just so darn painful.

PAWNOTE: I dread their visits. These strangers in blue overalls have had me locked in a cage for days now and every time they open the door, they hurt me. At first I was just very tired and confused but now I am recovering from my injuries and I recognise some faces and voices. Some of them come to put tubes in me and stick syringes full of drugs in my body but others clean my wounds. When they do that I try to bite them. I can tell I'm getting back to my old intolerant self, which must mean I'm getting better.

Today a man in a white coat removed the last tube from my leg wound. My back leg is in plaster and I can't move it at all and my tail is trussed up. I don't know what has gone on under that bandage but I could swear my swellegant, elegant tail is shorter than it was.

I am wearing a huge white collar that I imagine makes me look like an Elizabethan cat in a ruff, which I would hate another cat to see. I would be the laughing stock of the village. Obviously I must be recovering because I am now starting to take an interest in my appearance but the collar prevents me from turning round to clean my fur and it must be filthy by now. I have never been so dirty, not even when I was living rough. I smell quite unlike myself and it's making me unhappy.

My mistress has been in but she seems upset and I know I should be with her to comfort her. After all, that is my job. When she comes in she strokes my face but she cries all the time and then she goes away and leaves me at the mercy of these people. She talks constantly, too. I assume she is telling me her news but I can't whisk my tail like I normally do to tell her to shut up because it's wrapped up like a Christmas present and is too heavy to move in any direction. How will I ever jump onto the roof again and sit outside the bedroom window when her friends come to stay? One of them opened the curtains and called me a Peeping Tom once, which I rather resented but she thought was hysterically funny.

Today I have heard words like 'going home' being said and I hope it's me they're talking about. I have heard these words before but then other animals are reunited with their owners and I am left behind.

Then I hear a familiar voice. 'Is he ready to come with me?' she asks. I see her face peering into my cage. 'Gus, I'm here. We're going home but you have to be a very good cat.' I will be, I miaow at her, just take me with you this time, please don't leave me behind. She rubs my face, then my ears. 'I promise to give your coat a wash when we get home,' she says. 'I know how it must be distressing you to have a dirty coat. I can't use cat spit but I will use a cloth dampened with rainwater. Now, we're going to put you in a crate and lift it into the car. You're going to have to stay indoors in it for a while but you'll be fine. I'm looking after you now.'

I feel very insecure as I am carried in a

wobbling crate to her car and perched on the back seat, then strapped in with a belt. She can't get the roof of her car down with my cage in the back so the wind is in my fur as we drive back. It feels divine, whisking away the awful memories of the past week. The fresh air smells so good. I pick up the scent of grass and mice, foxes and rabbits, and I hear the birds singing ... oh, how I have missed the country. I've not been in a car for many years – I used all my wiles to persuade her that taking me to the vet in a cat basket wouldn't be a good idea for either of us, so she called the vet to me when I was bitten – but this is quite enjoyable.

I'm so looking forward to being back home. Back to some edible catfood, for one thing, that hospital food is such rubbish. I hope she has a good supply of my favourite food in, I need building up for I have become thin and scrawny while I've been shut in my cage. My muscles are quite wasted. I shall soon be up and about, climbing trees and terrorising any feathered and furry beasts that are smaller than me. We cats don't have time for self pity; as soon as we can move without too much pain we are back doing what we like doing best. In my case that will be eating, mousing and sleeping.

Now we are slowing down. I realise we are about to draw up at the kerb where I had my horrific accident when I hear my mistress shout, 'Excuse me, can you back up, please? I have a sick cat here and I need to go in that space,' and a man tooting his car horn and muttering, 'Silly cow.' I am home at last with the woman I love and all will be right with my world. Or will it? Has that dog gone or has she moved in in my absence? And what has happened with the man? Maybe it's not over yet.

Chapter Ten

Resolution is a Solution

Maisie had a black felt pen in her hand and bad thoughts on her mind after one too many ciders in The Bell. 'Now, how shall I change the village sign saying Cuckstone?' she thought. 'Change the C to an F or the u to an o?' Luckily at that point the postman cycled up the road.

'Not about to do something you might regret are you, Maisie?' he asked, staring first at her pen and then at the look on her face. She shook her head. It could wait. Probably best if it waited forever, actually. She'd never actually graffiti-ed anything but it wasn't for the lack of wanting to. Ever since she was a kid she'd yearned to put an i in the To Let signs she saw on the streets.

Tonight, though, she had wanted to let off a bit of steam. Life had been doling it out in spades recently, which was why she'd gone for a drink after visiting the post office. What with looking after Gus, trying to locate a new source of work before she went bankrupt and decide what to do about both Mike and Tom, she felt like a pressure cooker about to blow.

Gus was at home, still recovering from his injuries and in confinement at the cottage for at least another fortnight. She was not at all surprised to find he was the most impatient of patients, employing every wile he possessed to escape from his crate, and she had finally given in and let him out of it early. He cut a sad-looking figure compared to the sleek and sexy beast he'd been before his accident. His shaven fur had begun to grow back but it was patchy and uneven over the wounds and there were whole patches of white in it, rather than just the stray white hairs he'd had before. When he walked, his pinned leg caused him to limp and the tear in his back leg, although it was mending neatly, meant he could only jump stiffly onto chairs and tables.

Maisie had made some special beds for him on the floor around the house but he preferred to watch what was going on outside from a table or stool. He seemed reasonably happy to stay indoors but his relentless miaowing for her attention drove her mad when she was on the phone. She vowed to let him out for the first time as soon as he'd had his final check-up and X-rays at the hospital and the pin removed – a five minute procedure, she'd been told. She knew he would be a happier cat once he could sniff his way around familiar territory outside and she hoped it would help him regain his confidence.

Although it was probably the least of his problems, to Maisie the worst thing of all was the fact that his once graceful tail was now stunted, with a corkscrew-like bend in it. He'd actually only lost about three inches off it – less than Maisie had originally thought – but the tip had been squashed and was now raised in a semi-permanent question mark over his hairy rear end, giving him the look of a Disney cat. When she talked to him, he waved it but it didn't swish like before.

It was now over a month since Tom had stormed off. She had thought he would ring her in a day or two when he'd calmed down but he hadn't, and she couldn't ring him yet because she hadn't quite made up her mind. Mike had kept his promise, which surprised her, and hadn't contacted her either. And while she was pretty sure, deep down, that it was Tom she wanted to be with, the fact that he was keeping his distance was confusing her further.

As another week ground slowly by and he still didn't call her she decided she might as well meet up with Mike. What was the point in losing them both? If Tom was intending to dump her after they'd had their break, or maybe never even ring her again, then surely it was downright stupid to burn both her bridges at once. Mike was a good man, they just needed to spend a little time together to find out if they were still compatible. That would then give her a better idea of whether she could make a go of it with him, if Tom were to split up with her forever.

When she finally rang Mike he sounded delighted to hear from her. 'It's been ages since we met for lunch, Maisie. I was giving up hope,' he said, jovially. 'You never used to play this hard to get.'

'I'm not playing "to be got", Mike,' she said primly. 'I'm with Tom, remember?' But of course she wasn't, although she wasn't about to tell Mike that. Yet.

'So you've made up your mind, have you, and you're going to stay with your country vet?' said Mike.

'No, I haven't made up anything yet. I'm still in a complete muddle, if you really want to know, but it'd be nice to see you again.

Anyway, how are you coping with all the changes in your life?'

With a bit of fancy footwork she managed to get him talking about his pending divorce and how life was panning out in his new flat. After ten minutes or so they got round to arranging to meet when she was next in London.

'Maybe I can come down and visit you in the country soon, Maisie,' he added. His words sent a shudder through her. She didn't want him poking around her village just yet. It was still Tom territory.

'Maybe,' she said, non-commitally. 'We'll see, but please don't turn up unless I say so.'

By the time she met Mike again she was starting to waver over Tom. True, she hadn't called him and she could have done but then she hadn't been the one to suggest they had a trial separation and she hadn't been the one to walk out. A girl has her pride, she thought. If I go running to him he'll probably dismiss me, just like the last time. And Mike did look so very dashing, she thought with a pang of desire. He had that old-school charm to match his twinkling eyes and witty ways. For all his good points, nobody could ever say that Tom was a witty man. Funny, yes, but not sharp.

Mike and Maisie shared a bottle of champagne and then went on to eat in a Vietnamese restaurant. Maisie adored south-east Asian cuisine, there was something about the cool, fresh, limey, fishy, minty flavours, the hot chillies and the crispy vegetables that she couldn't get enough of. To start with they mainly discussed their problems with work and conversation was much easier than when they'd met in the Wine Press but over coffee, the talk turned, inevitably, to what Maisie was thinking about their future together.

'I simply don't know, Mike,' she said, frankly. 'I'm confused still. I love Tom and you've been out of my life for a long time now. I don't even know if we'd be compatible any more. I know I've changed and I'm sure you have, too. I owe it to Tom to try to work it out with him although I don't know how to.'

Unwisely, she told Mike what had happened and how Tom was ignoring her. It was far more than she meant to reveal to him but he was good at coaxing the truth from a reluctant subject.

'If only you'd come along six months ago things might have been different but I really can't start seeing you right now, the timing is terrible. Even if Tom and I were to split up I'd be devastated and in no fit state for another committed relationship, which is what I think you want, don't you?'

'I've only ever wanted you, Maisie, you know that,' he said. 'But it wasn't me who broke us up last time, was it? It was you.'

With a shudder she remembered back to that terrible time 13 years earlier. When Mike's wife discovered their affair he'd immediately said that he was staying with her. Maisie wasn't surprised – if the boot had been on the other foot she would have stayed with her family, too – but she was desperately upset when Mike said he'd told his wife their affair had already ended and if she contacted Maisie, would she please tell his wife the same story. He begged Maisie to lie for him and like an idiot she said she would, although luckily she had never had to. But she'd never forgotten that he did that to her ... that one demand of his seemed to contradict all his protestations of love, and his agonising over which woman he wanted to spend the rest of his life with. Eventually, after they'd drifted along joylessly for months making each other increasingly unhappy, Maisie said she wasn't going to see him any more. Mike had found this hard to take – he'd become unattractively needy, calling her at all hours, turning up on her doorstep, even threatening to kill himself at one point.

'But you want your cake and you want to eat it, too,' Maisie remembered telling him. 'You can't have me and your wife and children, it's not possible for any of us to go on like that. You've chosen to be with them, not me. That has to be the end of it. I can't do this any more.' To the hauntingly pertinent strains of Ella Fitzgerald singing 'Ev'ry Time We Say Goodbye', she pushed him out of the door of her London flat. Both of them were crying. Did she really want to go through that again? The answer had to be no. And yet ... she couldn't deny that there was still something between them.

Maisie sensibly ended the evening without drinking herself into a situation she'd later regret but she did arrange to speak to Mike again the following week. Then the phone calls started. She'd forgotten about this side of him, how he used to ring her incessantly. Their affair took place in those halcyon days before most people had mobiles and were constantly available but even so, he used to bombard her with messages on her answer phones at home and work. Once she'd been in the middle of a call to a friend and he said afterwards he'd tried her 20 times. He was a bit of a control freak, she'd realised at the time, and it seemed that some things never changed.

Meanwhile, Gus had at last been given a clean bill by the animal hospital and Maisie had let him out into the garden. The weather that October was balmy and beautiful and he spent his days lazing on the lawn in the sun, his black ears turning pink in the heat. His injuries were healing much faster now and he wasn't as stiff as he had been. He'd even jumped over the wall and brought her back a mouse the other day, which she'd captured alive in her bare hands – she was adept at this now – and rehabilitated in her moss-lined mouse box at the back of the garden.

Out of the blue, she got a call from a publisher she knew. 'Would you like to come and meet me for lunch, Maisie?' said Carla. 'I've got something I'd like to discuss with you. I need a ghost-writer for a biography we're thinking of publishing and I thought of you straight away. There won't be a huge amount of money in it but I could give you a small advance and it should bring you in a bit once it's out.'

Maisie couldn't believe her luck. Ghostwriting would be right up her street. Hadn't she spent the past 25 years interviewing people about their lives? Maybe this meant her luck was changing at last. It was about time, it had been a pretty rotten few weeks.

She was becoming sick of worrying about what to do about Tom and Mike and had realised she was beginning to enjoy the single life again. Being in a couple wasn't all it was cracked up to be. Having her double bed to herself for the past six weeks was a treat she'd really missed when she was with Tom – he'd taken up a lot of room – and it was nice to be able to cuddle up to Gus again at nights. She could choose what she ate and when and who she mixed with. She didn't have to keep meeting up with Tom's boring, sporty, drinking chums – and, she supposed, he didn't keep having to meet her boozy, celebrity-obsessed journalist mates. You did a lot of compromising when you were with someone, she rationalised, but where was that final certainty that told you it was worth the sacrifice of giving up your independence? Being single was a very 21st century way of living and with more single person households than ever before, it was becoming more acceptable. She had lost count of the number of articles she'd written about the pros and cons of single life over the years and until recently she'd seen more cons than pros.

Now she had her chance not to be single any more, which is what she thought she wanted, but this business with Tom had shaken her faith in romance. She'd always believed that if she loved someone and they loved her then anything was possible but in this instance that wasn't working. And she was still being pulled emotionally by Mike. The time has come, she told herself, to resolve this once and for all. The problem is, how? She needed something to happen to force her to decide.

Instead of dithering over her love life, she threw herself into her work, reading and researching the synopsis and chapter breakdown for her book. It was fascinating stuff – the subject of the book, one of the early feminists, was dead, so she spent hours trawling through online information on the suffragettes and was blown away by their courage. What enraged her was that less than 100 years ago the Pankhurst sisters and other women had paid with their lives to get the right to vote, yet she'd heard so many women today say they 'couldn't be bothered' to get themselves down to the polling booth. We've become a very spoiled nation, she thought, spoon-fed and over-privileged, with little understanding of true values.

As she pondered how quickly we forget, there was a knock at her door. She peered down from her office. It looked like Mike. What was he doing here?

'I need to talk to you, Maisie,' he began, as he stepped into the porch. 'I keep ringing you and you don't ring me back. What's going on? Why are you ignoring me?'

There had always been a last-straw-on-the-camel's-back point with Maisie and this was it. She hated emotional blackmail.

'Come in, Mike, and have a cuppa. I've been trying to work out this one out and I think you turning up today – when I asked you not to – has just solved my dilemma.'

He looked startled. 'Don't say I've blown it by coming to visit you in the sticks. I thought you'd be pleased to see me. I took the day off especially to take you away from the boredom of your working day and buy you lunch at one of your local-yokel hostelries.'

The sticks. Local-yokel hostelries. It was suddenly crystal clear to her that Mike and she were incompatible. He hated the country, she loved it. He was trying to win her back now, but what for? It wouldn't bring either of them happiness. She was never going to return to live in London and he was uncomfortable with the lack of shops and fancy restaurants, the mud and general rawness of rural life. Added to that, he'd done the one thing she'd asked him not to do – come and visit her. Tom on the other hand had kept his distance, he hadn't pestered her even though she'd have appreciated a bit of pestering from him, and, like her, he loved the Sussex countryside. In a sudden flash, she knew for certain that it was Tom she wanted to be with. They had a future, if only she could resurrect it. She and Mike, however, did not.

She sat him down at her circular dining table with a cup of steaming hazelnut coffee – her current favourite – and looked at him hard. 'Mike, listen to me. I'm going to say this just once. It's not going to work between us. We're chalk and cheese. That didn't matter all those years ago – I was living in London, so were all my friends, and we enjoyed every second of it at that time. All the late-night drinking and partying, going out for meals in flash restaurants, seeing West End plays and new films the second they came out was great fun – but that was then and this is now. I haven't changed in who I am but I have changed in what I want. I'm older now and I've found that what makes me happy is a quieter, less ambitious, less flamboyant, life.

'You want us to be back where we were 13 years ago but I can't do that. You'd hate to live here – you've just demonstrated that by the way you talk about my life, as if it's an indulgence and I need my head patted by sensible, paternal you. You don't know what makes me tick any more but I'm telling you: this does. My life here in Cuckstone is good. I don't want to live amidst the sirens and fumes, constantly looking over my shoulder to see if someone's about to mug me. I want to live among people who care when you're ill or work is crap and for the first time in my life I've found a place where I can settle, somewhere that I can call home. That to me is worth more than a romance with someone I once loved, because I'm afraid that's how I feel. I don't love you any more and we don't have a future together. I'm sorry. I didn't mean to mislead you.'

She stopped. That phrase about a load being lifted off your back was true, she felt light as a feather suddenly. I've done the right thing, she thought to herself. Now, I need to concentrate all my energies on getting Tom back.

Mike was speaking. 'Actually, Maisie, I came to take you out to lunch to tell you that I've met someone else. It's early days yet and she's much younger than me – half my age, in fact – but she's gorgeous and a really promising news reporter. She lives in London and I think we have a future. I wanted to break it to you gently. I, too, could see it probably wouldn't work between us any more and you being so unsure for so long just confirmed it. You're a different animal now and we want different things but I'd like us to stay friends. Do you think that's possible? And are you going to go back to Tom?'

Maisie had had all the wind removed from her sails and was sitting with her mouth open. He'd found someone else *already?* How did men do that? They were never on their own for long – they probably couldn't manage without a woman to do their washing and shopping – yet women like herself were on their own for years, struggling along. It was so unfair! And his new bit was younger, much younger, and gorgeous – and a 'promising news reporter', like she herself once had been. Despite what she'd decided, Maisie could feel herself getting itchy with jealousy. She was also extremely embarrassed.

'I'm sorry, Mike,' she stuttered. Then she caught his eye. 'God, we're both as bad as each other,' she said. 'I guess we can stay friends. It's none of my business but I don't think you're ready for another committed relationship yet, you've probably got some grieving to do over your wife, though I wish you all the best. As for me ... yes, I'm going to give it my absolute best shot with Tom. If nothing else good has come of us this time round, that has. I know now that he's the one for me. Now I just have to find out a way to get him back.'

Mike stood up and gave her a peremptory hug. 'Well, good luck, Maisie. I think we'll skip the lunch, but thanks for everything. You take care now, and keep in touch. Promise?'

She hugged him back. 'Promise.'

She closed the door behind him and went over to Gus, who was lying in a patch of sunlight on the kitchen table. 'Guess what, beastie boy?' she said. 'I'm going to get Tom back. You'll approve of that, won't you?' She stroked his ears as he purred. Yes, it seemed he approved. 'The only problem is, how? Got any suggestions?'

Maisie spent the afternoon trying to concentrate on her biography but after achieving precisely nothing she gave up and went out for a walk. After climbing to the top of the Downs and back she found herself outside Lucy's house. Her mind was clear.

'Lucy, are you home?' she yelled. 'I have to talk to you.'

'I'm here, Maisie, in the garden behind the privet bush. There's no need to shout,' said Lucy. 'You've made up your mind, I take it. What did you decide?'

'I want Tom,' announced Maisie, and explained what had happened with Mike. 'The problem is, I don't know how to get him back. You have to help.'

'Hmm, this could be tricky,' said Lucy. 'I was wondering how to tell you this but I saw Tom in the pub last night with another woman. I don't know who she was but at one point he had his arm round her. You need to get a move on if you're not going to lose him once and for all. Now, this is what I suggest ...'

An hour later, Maisie was on her way home. She raced into her office and pulled out a large roll of lining paper, a pair of scissors, a tape measure, a roll of Sellotape and a thick red felt pen and spent the evening cutting, pasting and sticking. First thing the next morning she rang the local florist and placed an order for a huge bunch of sunflowers, the happiest flowers she knew, to be sent to Tom's home address with a note. It read: 'Please go to the top of Long Hill as soon as possible and look down at my office.' She knew he'd know who it was from.

Then she sat in her office, bit her nails and waited. And waited. And waited. All day. Of course she hadn't expected Tom to be at home on a Tuesday but why did the man have to work such long hours? And would her ploy succeed?

Soon after six o'clock, when she thought she'd die if she had to wait any longer, she saw a man in a stripy blue rugby shirt climb the hill. As he reached the summit she saw him turn towards her house, lean forwards a bit, do a kind of doubletake - and then run down the hill. He'd obviously seen her message:

TOM
I
LOVE
YOU

in huge red letters that she'd cut out and pasted to the panes of her office window.

'Please, God, let him be running towards me and not away from me,' prayed Maisie.

The next minute there was a bang on the door.

'Maisie, Maisie, let me in,' he cried. 'You daft idiot, I love you too.' He flung his arms around her. 'Why didn't you ring me? I've been waiting for your call for weeks. I've missed you so much.'

'I've missed you, too, Tom,' she said, tears spilling down her face. 'I'm so desperately sorry. I was so confused and it took me ages to sort things out in my head. After you'd walked out on me I thought you didn't want to know and then it all got into an even worse muddle. But it's you I want to be with, you and nobody else. I know that beyond a shadow of a doubt, it just took me a while. But why didn't you ring me? I thought you were furious with me.'

'I was, at first, then I thought you were going back to Mike and that was what you'd always wanted and I didn't want to stand in your way but I couldn't bear it,' Tom gabbled. 'I didn't ring because if you'd told me it was over I couldn't have coped. I figured it was better not to know, so I buried myself in work and just kept hoping that one day you'd put me out of my misery.'

'But Lucy saw you in the pub with another woman, you had your arm round her,' blurted out Maisie. 'I thought you'd found somebody else.'

He kissed her – and then he kissed her again. 'Maisie, you are the love of my life and I don't want anybody else but you. I have to confess ... I was so desperate I went to see Lucy and we cooked that one up between us. I was hoping it would make up your mind for you. I think it worked, don't you?'

'Tom, I'd made up my mind before that. I just had to be sure that I had totally laid the past to rest and I have. Mike is out of my life and you are in it. But I think we have a lot to talk about...'

They spent the rest of the evening hugging and kissing and discussing what they'd been doing over the past few weeks.

'Tom, don't take this the wrong way but I think we rushed things,' said Maisie, much later, from the comfort of her double bed. It might have been nice to sleep alone but it was fantastic to have him back in it again.

'I don't think either of us is ready to move in together yet. We know what it's like to be together and we know we don't want to be apart. Can we just stay as we were for a bit? Gus and Tosca will never be able to live together and this is the only solution that will work but they're also both getting on a bit and, although it's awfully sad to think about, one day we won't have them. I've never been one for convention – I've done a lot of thinking recently and I quite like having my space to myself most of the time and it's also what I'm used to. Living apart but spending most of our spare time together worked before. Would you be happy to see if we can make it work again? It doesn't need to mean we're less committed to one another, just that we're not following the normal path of living together and marriage.'

'Maisie, I agree,' replied Tom, rolling over onto his back. 'I'd come to much the same conclusion myself. After my marriage ended it took me a long time to get back on my feet, both financially and emotionally, and although I love you to bits I'm not sure I want to be that vulnerable ever again. Like you, I've created a haven for myself at home and I like being there. If you're happy, then I'm happy. Let's leave it at that and enjoy what we've got, because we so very nearly lost each other. And Gussie.'

There was a little 'ow?' from the foot of the bed and Gus landed squarely on Tom's stomach. 'Phooff, you weigh a ton, cat. I can see you're better,' he said. 'You know, Maisie, he's never done that before. I think he's glad to see us back together again.'

PAWNOTE: You must be joking, pal. You're better than the other men she's picked but you don't own her and you never will. Not while I'm around, anyway. People under-estimate us cats and long may they continue to do so. It works in our favour. They think we're sweet and fluffy but we're not. We have an iron will and manipulative ways and we don't give up easily. If I hadn't rushed out of that door and run under the car then my mistress might now be living with the man and his detestable dog and I would have been forced to leave the place I've made my home.

Of course, I've paid a huge price for my continued security. My tail, my beautiful tail that was my pride and joy will never be the same again, but I use it, and my other injuries, to good effect. She will never forget what she and the man put me through. Speak to me in a cross voice and they will see me feebly attempt to wave my tail. Order me off the dining table, where I love to lounge in the sun, and she will see me limp. These are useful tools and elicit sympathy every time I invoke them. She is a fool but she is the fool I choose to share my life with and I am fond of her. More than fond. She is my everything.

Every day I creep up the long, dark alley between the two houses and hide in the dense rhododendron bushes at the back of the garden, where I watch her movements with my grape-green eyes. My life is good. I have retained the love of the woman I wanted, I am still the man of the house and I have an endless supply of birds and mice to daily with. What more could one cat want?